WREN JANE BEACON AT WAR

BOOK TWO:
SURVIVAL

A NOVEL BY
DJ Lindsay

See also Book One, 'Wren Jane Beacon Goes to War'

www.wrenjaneb.co.uk

A CIP catalogue record for this book is available from the British Library.

Book cover design: Alan Cooper, www.alancooperdesign.co.uk

A note on character

All the main protagonists in this story are fictitious. It is a novel set in a particular time, when large personalities at the top of organisations inevitably have a bearing on the story being told. Rather than invent spurious personalities these people are named and involved in the story. I have tried to be true to their character, as far as can be told from the written record. I have also worked on the basis of only invoking real people when it is possible to be positive and attribute good characteristics. The unpleasant and bad characters that arise are fictitious. They may reflect particular attitudes of that time and of types of personality, but have no links to any particular person, living or dead.

Retrospective

Wren Jane Beacon at War; Survival is the second book in the series following the eponymous heroine when she joins the Women's Royal Naval Service (WRNS) at the start of World War Two in 1939. Book One '*Wren Jane Beacon goes to War; In the Beginning*' follows her adventures in boats in the early days of the conflict and through her time rescuing soldiers on the beaches of Dunkirk. Badly wounded, she brings her battered boat back to Dover, only to find she is in serious trouble with the Naval authorities, having defied direct orders not to go. Book Two is well named '*Survival*' as she recovers from her wounds, both inner and outer, emotional and physical and a fierce argument is raging about her presence at the front line and her clearly heroic actions. As a result, she becomes more reflective about war and her place in it.

Book One describes how this spirited girl has already been through many challenges. With a background in yachting to her early days as a deckhand on a Naval launch at Devonport she learns her trade. To understand the Royal Navy she is sent on the Wrens Probationer Course, where the traumas and demands see her give and receive rough handling. But with her catchphrase, "I will not be defeated" and her fierce willpower, all is overcome. Book One ends when she is in the English Channel in her Naval launch and features the many seamanship challenges encountered during the voyage.

Being a lively young lady her emotional life is never far away and she takes her first lover – a French Naval officer – at an early stage. In 1939, this was a daring action and being found out lands her in deep trouble with the Wren authorities. It is only her brilliance at the job and her bravery in saving her launch's Cox'n from drowning, which rescues her from being dismissed from the service. Through Book One and up to the end of Book Two, she accumulates the most lurid disciplinary record in Wren history.

Find out more at www.wrenjaneb.co.uk

Acknowledgements

During the eight years of writing Books One and Two, a wide range of people provided support and contributions; they have inspired the book series and I thank them, most sincerely. The two books are closely intertwined and those people who helped with Book One were also contributing to Book Two at the same time.

These include: Peter Leppard, the book's best friend; Glenda Whitley, ex-Wren, Sea Cadet Officer and keen sailor and boat person, who informed the books on all matters Wren and ceremonial; Caroline Anns Baldock, who advised on literary aspects; at some times Jennifer Russell, Jessica Smith and in the early stages Dr Jo Stanley.

Three established authors, Richard Woodman, Sam Llewellyn and Frank Welsh were supportive with their comments as was the tough professional approach provided by the Hillary Johnson Authors' Advisory Service, which helped the story to be completed.

Alan Cooper Design has performed his magic on taking the bare text and turning it into a published book.

I also thank Yvonne Downer, a delightful 94-year-old lady who I had the privilege to meet. She had been a boat crew Wren in World War Two in *HMS Tormentor*, on the River Hamble.

Thanks also to my literary agent and editor, Wendy Yorke, who has contributed hugely to bringing the story to a published book standard, while inspiring me to continue writing the rest of the series.

Dedications

To my beta critics who have kept the faith.

Contents

Prologue 8

PART ONE: DOVER 11
    CHAPTER 1: On the Mend 13
    CHAPTER 2: Settling In 18
    CHAPTER 3: Onto the Boats 23
    CHAPTER 4: The Shadows Lengthen 30
    CHAPTER 5: Decision Time 39

PART TWO: RECOVERY 45
    CHAPTER 6: The Convalescent 47
    CHAPTER 7: Tribunal 52
    CHAPTER 8: Troughs and Peaks 58
    CHAPTER 9: Persuasion 64

PART THREE: HOME FIRES BURNING 67
    CHAPTER 10: The Haunting Past 68
    CHAPTER 11: Family Connections 75
    CHAPTER 12: Thinking 81

PART FOUR: UNDER THE BATTLE 89
    CHAPTER 13: Going Up 91
    CHAPTER 14: Old and New 100
    CHAPTER 15: Picking Up 107
    CHAPTER 16: Highs and Lows 113
    CHAPTER 17: The Complexities of Life 120

PART FIVE: LONDON 129
    CHAPTER 18: Before the King 131
    CHAPTER 19: At First Sight 140
    CHAPTER 20: The Lion's Den 147
    CHAPTER 21: The Real Thing 152

GLOSSARY 159
BIBLIOGRAPHY 165
About the Author 169

Prologue

In 1940, with the might of the German war machine roaring at them the British people stood firm and refused to be defeated. Inspired by Churchill's oratory, the British shook a defiant fist at Hitler, giving the nation a self-belief which never left it. In my trade as a journalist I had listened to many remarkable stories; 'The people' is after all, only the sum of its individuals and their stories were the sum of that refusal to give in. One of the most remarkable stories I heard was that of Wren Jane Beacon who took a boat to the Hell of Dunkirk, did great things with it and survived to tell the tale. Twenty years old when she went, by the time I got to listen to her story in 1944, she was a battle-scarred Chief Wren with a steely inner strength. Getting her to start telling her story was not easy but once she did it poured out. In one of our later debriefings I asked, "After those great days on the beaches of Dunkirk, life can never have been quite the same, I would imagine?"

"Yes and no. It was certainly a life-changing experience and whatever fear I had of dying went then. I was never a carefree kid again that is for sure, but even so I had the resilience of youth, so the toughening up I got didn't stop me wanting to dance or have a good time. It is awfully easy to get warped by something like that and I have seen veterans who never really got over it or enjoyed life again. But three things stopped me getting too case hardened and miserable: one, the war went on and I had my place in it as a pioneer boat Wren, a huge and exciting challenge. Two, no rough experience can take away the sheer joy of being in a boat, out on the water, at dawn. You can't help feeling deeply conscious of our endless capacity to rise again like the sun and that really is life affirming. Thirdly, I fell in love and for a while I felt utterly invincible."

"Yes, but on those beaches you demonstrated a courage and ability way up there with any of our great heroes and you must know it."

She snorted. "Pah. Tell that to their lordships. There are still people at the top would have me dismissed in disgrace tomorrow if they could. These medals weren't given entirely voluntarily, you know. That stops you getting inflated ideas about how special you are."

"One of these days you'll be recognised."

"That's all very well but surely you know by now that I didn't do it to be recognised or told how wonderful I am. It was because it needed doing and here I am, 'still knocking around and still just a Wren'. The fact that I nearly died was incidental."

More widely, by spring 1940 the Royal Navy had already been involved in a series of major actions and the gearing up to cope with the multitude of demands on it was bearing fruit. Although it had sustained serious losses it had also had several important victories and its presence was spreading ever wider.

Jane looked at me thoughtfully. "What I hadn't realised when I arrived in Dover after that all-engrossing voyage up Channel in Amaryllis, was that a large part of the Navy was taken up with the Norwegian campaign. Because the Navy won that war on the water, exemplified by the battleship Warspite's charge into Narvik Fjord to sink German destroyers, I only saw later what a grossly misjudged event the Norwegian campaign was."

I cut in. "Yes it was bizarre: the British seemed to think that a strong naval presence could defeat the blitzkrieg which had ripped through Denmark and Norway in a matter of days. Without adequate air cover the Army could do little except try to protect itself and the whole sad adventure was doomed with the German forces firmly in control."

Jane nodded. "At the time, it seemed like a complete disaster but as I understand it in the end there was one benefit from the fiasco. Although the Luftwaffe and German Army might have been overwhelmingly victorious, the German Navy took a real beating. It lost a heavy cruiser, ten heavy destroyers, which was half its strength of them, two light cruisers, nine submarines and a torpedo boat. In addition, six more of its heavy ships were badly mauled and not available for action for some time."

I was startled to hear Jane quoting statistics at me. By 1944, she clearly had studied the Navy's war more than she sometimes admitted. But there was another dimension to this story, which she hadn't mentioned. Although far from the only reason, the lack of German surface ships in a fit condition was a significant factor in calling off Operation Sealion, the planned invasion of Britain in autumn 1940. Thanks to the battering they had been given in the Narvik campaign, the Kreigsmarine could not provide adequate sea forces to protect the crossing invasion force within any timetable acceptable to Hitler or the Wehrmacht. This was a fortuitous side-effect far from the planners' minds when they went into Norway, but Britain survived at that time by a series of chance occurrences, which favoured it.

Jane smiled. "Yes, we were really very lucky at that time. There was little us just hanging on and doing our jobs. We managed to scrape through but it really was very tense for a while. Dover was on edge the whole time."

Listening to Jane, I could hear how much of a war area she had sailed into in the spring of 1940. Plymouth might have been busy but Dover buzzed, its frontline position making it a critical hinge in the nation's sea defences. The sense of being on the front line was strong. The twenty-one miles of sea separating it from the Continent was a narrow but crucial moat. In the course of World War Two, Dover would be bombed, shelled from France, have E-boats rip through the harbour at speed firing wildly and have mines laid up to its entrance, but it remained an active and viable harbour throughout the war. The narrow seas — the area from Southern North Sea through the Dover Strait to West

English Channel – were to be fought over continuously for the next five years. It took the Royal Navy most of those years to get on top of their enemies in fiercely contested small unit warfare.

"Jane, this strategy is fascinating but it's a long way from your own story. Can we get back to that, please? Last I heard of your recovery from your Dunkirk wounds, you were in a hospital bed with a very uncertain future. Can we pick it up again from there?"

She smiled, that sad lop-sided smile driven by the experiences of front line war.

PART ONE:

DOVER

CHAPTER 1:
On the Mend

Ensconced in the comfort of her hospital bed and recovering well from her Dunkirk wounds, it took some time for Jane Beacon to tell her psychiatrist the story of her time in the Wrens from joining until she got to Dover, but it was a straightforward tale with only a few serious hiccups. The beaches of Dunkirk and the faces, which caused her such nightmares, were a more difficult process.

Jane had started rambling on about The Emperor and what a lovely donkey he was, which took even a psychiatrist like Mrs Goodall some time to disentangle and make sense of. From there Jane regressed to the groping soldiers and shuddered at the memory all over again.

"Faces, hands, and pain. That's what it was all about."

"So, the bombs and shells didn't worry you so much?"

"Oh, they were the backdrop to it all. If they got you, you were a-gonner and as long as they didn't you got on with the job."

"But you were wounded. Didn't that bother you?"

"I can't pretend I liked it but that's the price of going there."

Her voice rose as she spoke. Again she was trembling, shaking her head and beating it feebly with clenched fists. "It was the people, the dead bodies, the faces, the hands, the stink, the madmen and the sad desperate ones. That's what gets to you. And loose heads. That was horrible."

"I imagine it was. Now, can you put your Dunkirk time in some sort of order?"

Jane suddenly slumped. "Not today. Can we try again another time?"

"Yes, Miss Beacon, we can. My time's up anyway. I will come back tomorrow and we'll see if we can help you handle these memories so you can live with them."

Jane collapsed back against the pillows, utterly drained. They tried a lighter sleeping pill that night and although the faces came back it was not as stark as the night before. But her sleep was not good. Next day, Mrs Goodall came for a longer session through the morning and managed to get a coherent story out of Jane, who felt lighter, more at ease by the end. Mrs Goodall reported to the medical staff at lunchtime; in her opinion Jane was young enough and resilient enough to come to terms with her memories. "What she really needs is something else to engage her mind. I'd recommend getting her looking at the wider world again as soon as possible." The young Lieutenant junior doctor seemed noticeably keen on the idea of spending some time with Jane. "Remember the rest of your patients as well," cautioned the Commander. But soon after lunch his junior appeared at Jane's bedside and casually asked, "Have you been following the war and events?"

Jane shook her head. "Not since the evacuation. How's the war going?"

"Well, France is collapsing rapidly and we don't think it will hold out for more than a week or two now. The last British troops are in the West of France and being evacuated as we speak. Mr Churchill has promised us that we'll fight on alone, but there's a strong feeling that if the Boche choose to come across the Channel there's not a lot we can do to stop them. The sooner you're fit again the better."

Jane laughed, her first outright burst of amusement for a long time. "Why, am I to fight them off singlehanded?"

"Not entirely, but we need everyone possible." He looked into her smiling eyes and a spark of mutual contact flowed between them. "Have you any interests? Can I get you anything to read?"

"Well, I like French literature and I've promised myself to learn something about the Navy."

"I don't know about French literature but I'm into Naval history myself. We've a good stock of Naval books in the wardroom. Perhaps I can borrow a couple of them for you to read, then we can discuss them."

Jane smiled into his eyes. "Yes, that would be nice."

After he had left, whistling tunelessly, Jane felt much bucked up.

Despite this, she kept having little relapses when the faces reared up in front of her again; at one stage the French Lieutenant's head rolled out from under her bed and she screamed in terror. When the staff came running she wailed, "He's there, he's there, under the bed."

"Who, Miss Beacon?"

"Lieutenant LeMaitre of course, can't you see him?"

"Now, now, he's not really there. It's only your imagination."

"But I saw his head just now, same as at the battery."

Mrs Goodall was summoned and in her quietly expert way got Jane talking about the expedition to the battery and how the stray mortar round had killed so many people, and all about her coming-to on the bottom boards with the head staring at her. "Well, Miss Beacon, that must have been horrible but he's gone now and isn't really under the bed. If I hold your hand you can get out of bed and see for yourself."

Having satisfied herself the Lieutenant or his head weren't there, Jane collapsed on the bed, wailing softly. "He was a nice man, really. Deserved better than having his head blown off."

"I'm sure he did but that's war I'm afraid. If you're going to put yourself in the front line you must expect that."

"Must I really? Oh well, maybe." And with that she fell back on the pillows and was instantly asleep. A blanket was spread over her and the nursing staff kept a close eye on her until the next day. She had a better night's sleep and although the faces came back and she moaned and whimpered in her sleep, it was nothing like as bad. She woke feeling refreshed for the first time in days. Sister Donaldson carried out her early morning checks and nodded approvingly. "You seem to be staging a rapid recovery. That's good."

Then, the young Lieutenant doctor came by with a couple of books, one light and full of pictures, the other a solid tome on the Royal Navy since 1750. He also brought the previous day's *Times* with apologies for it being out of date. "Not half as out of date as I am." She looked at the date: 15th June. "Goodness me. I hadn't realised I had been out of commission for so long. It only feels like a few days since I left for the beaches. What have I been doing?"

"Lying in a coma, then slowly coming together again. I don't think you realise how near death you were when you arrived here. We don't really understand how you survived. But I must get on." And with a nod he was gone. But his five minutes at her bedside had put a sparkle in Jane's eyes.

* * *

What Jane didn't know was that during her four days of being unconscious in hospital, a fierce debate had blown up about her. A certain senior Admiral had decreed that she was to be dismissed from the service immediately, as a disciplinary principle. When General Brownlow, who she had rescued from La Panne, heard of this he was appalled. "Buffy, you can't dismiss this girl. She saved me, and thousands of my men, including a section of rear guard extracted under fire. One of my Regimental Sergeant Majors was hugely impressed by her guts and determination. I'll have her in the Auxiliary Territorial Service (ATS, the Army's Women's Service) as a war heroine tomorrow if you throw her out. But what a waste; she's brilliant with boats."

"This war hero you describe, disobeyed direct orders twice, went absent without leave and took Admiralty property without permission. Am I supposed to condone that?"

"Nelson disobeyed orders to be a hero, Buffy."

"This girl is not Nelson and I'm damned if I'll have the comparison. You're not serious about taking her into the ATS surely?"

"I most certainly am. If you'd been there at midnight with explosions all around and people dying under your feet and seen her, cool as they come, you'd not be condemning her either."

"Well, she's not to be made a heroine."

"If she comes to us she will be. I'm putting her up for an Army medal anyway, which is within my powers to do. You must choose for yourself."

"That's blackmail and I'm damned if I'll have it." The senior Admiral banged the desk, went puce and glowered at his counterpart, but felt a singular helplessness about the whole business.

This was not helped when the Report of Proceedings landed on his desk from a young, but well-connected Lieutenant Commander from a ship sunk at Dunkirk. Along with the dry reportage on the loss of the ship bombed to the seabed, there was fulsome praise for the young Wren who had rescued them. "She showed extreme bravery in bringing her cutter in through the wall of flames, putting it alongside and taking us all off, including the two wounded men. Without this intervention there is no doubt we would all have died." Even through the stilted prose of the formal report admiration shone through. Normally such praise was an automatic step to an award.

Also, a letter of thanks and appreciation from the army nursing service, the QAIMNS, had been forwarded to the Admiral from the Admiralty, full of praise for the Wren's initiative and ability to command the troops. This was not well received. He was puzzled by being handed a photograph of a donkey, until that little story was explained by the Captain of the tug, and a letter of thanks was forwarded from the India Office. This was all getting too ridiculous. To balance it, the report from Beach Master Commander Leslie, taking its cue from the Admiral's views, was less friendly. 'Brave but difficult, argumentative, and too pushy' was how Jane was described. The Admiral liked that one.

Then, the French Admirals and Generals got on to him, babbling away in fractured English about the wonderful girl who had rescued them. "We give her big medals, for sure," the senior French Admiral promised. "Bloody Frogs" was the senior British Admiral's only comment after they'd left.

A certain Rear-Admiral Rodmayne had kept his distance during this argument, although his sense of pride was profound. Then he went to see his counterpart, one rank above him so within reach and admitted that her presence was his fault. This did not play well. The senior Admiral was no admirer of women usurping men's jobs and the suggestion that her behaviour only confirmed their suitability got a frosty reception. "Why do we need these damn females at all?" he snarled.

"Because we've a desperate manpower shortage and every female who can do something like this releases a man for the fleet. You must have seen the posters?"

"Well yes, but that's only for some fun for the boys. Surely, you're not suggesting they can do a serious job?"

"I most certainly am and I think that this confirms it."

"I'll not have it, damn you. This is a man's world and should stay that way. Have you gone soft or something?"

Now this pair had been Captain and Commander on a cruiser on the China station during troubled times and had seen several interesting skirmishes together, so there was mutual respect beneath the differences of viewpoint. Rear-Admiral Rodmayne left his opinion in writing with the secretary, as was his entitlement.

None of this crossfire played as strongly in the Admiral's mind as the disobedience, but then he found himself under sniper fire from Wren Head Quarters. Someone there was pushing Jane's case. They acknowledged her disobedience and confirmed that a penalty was called for, but suggested that it had been for a good cause and that dismissal was a peculiarly cruel form of acknowledgement. After losing his temper with all around him, banging the desk and swearing at the cat, the senior Admiral snarled, "Form a tribunal, haul her before it as soon as she's fit, and let them decide. You can put on the table my opinion that she should be heaved out." His secretary smiled a very secretarial smile and went off to organise it.

* * *

Jane was feeling better by the day and at rounds the next morning the Commander checked her over, nodded with satisfaction. "We'll be moving you up to the Wrennery sick bay later today. Be ready to move mid-afternoon," he said.

"Yes sir. Will medical staff and Mrs Goodall be able to visit me there?"

"Yes of course. Once you're out of our acute unit we will encourage you to have visitors of all sorts. How are the ribs?"

"Not too bad if I'm careful but sudden movements don't half hurt."

"Well, that's not surprising. Another couple of weeks and they'll be well on the way to knitting together and the pain should rapidly die down. But don't overdo it meantime, or you might open them up again."

The rest of the morning was taken up with another session with Mrs Goodall.

"Miss Beacon, I've heard about your progress until you arrived at Dover and about your exploits at Dunkirk, but there's a gap in between. Can you tell me about that?"

"If you wish, but that period was fairly humdrum, simply getting settled in and into the way of doing things at Dover, which was very different from Plymouth."

"Even so I'd like to know about. There might be clues to why you went to Dunkirk at all."

CHAPTER 2:
Settling In

When the launch *Amaryllis* arrived at Dover in mid-April 1940 from Plymouth after the tough trip up-channel, Wren Jane Beacon looked round from its deck. She saw the harbour full of elderly destroyers, trawlers taken over and converted to minesweepers along with drifters being used in many roles and even a flotilla of paddle steamers converted to minesweepers. Apart from the Navy, the port's main activities were still its classic ones. In the entrance *Amaryllis* had to dodge a charging ferry carrying men and supplies to France. The Navy was using the port to patrol the straight, along with a great deal of mine laying and minesweeping. The first few coastal forces motor gunboats were appearing, but they were still embryonic.

Once *Amaryllis* had tied up in the boats area outside Granville Dock, her Cox'n Stan Roberts reported to the boats officer, taking Jane with him. The reception was cool. "For a start you are seven days overdue. Your Admiral has been getting very cross not having his boat available and mostly we've been in the dark about your whereabouts. This will not continue. The boat's primary use will be to serve Rear-Admiral Rodmayne's needs but you will be under my control and you must understand that."

Chief Petty Officer Stan Roberts, with twenty-five years in the Navy under his belt, had not expected anything else and simply came to attention with a "Yes sir."

"As for you, young lady...."

This was a form of address Jane Beacon was getting fairly used to. "As for you, I'm less than convinced by this so-called experiment of having women crewing on the harbour boats, but I have clear orders to give it a try and therefore will do so. But it's up to you to convince me that you can do the job." Jane imitated Stan by coming to attention and saying, "Yes sir."

"Another thing, Cox'n Roberts will stay with his boat, as will the Stoker, but in general we run the boat crew ratings on a pool system, which means you can be assigned to any boat any day. Can you cope with that?"

"I don't see why not, sir. We're a very strong team on *Amaryllis*, which I'll miss, but wider experience will probably do me good. Do the other boats crew here know about my coming?"

"Oh yes, there's been too much chat by half already. I'll say no more at this stage. For today, you can get yourselves into quarters and settled. I'll expect you here at the office tomorrow morning at 0630. Carry on."

They both saluted and backed out. "Bit of a stickler" muttered Jane as they walked back. "Oh, I don't know. About typical, I'd say," said Stan, offhandedly. Walking down the jetty they met Rear-Admiral Rodmayne coming the other way. His eyes lit up, returning salute on seeing them. "Ah, you've finally arrived. That's good. You can take me out to the *Keith* lying on the trots." So, they turned round, started up and made their first run. The Admiral called Jane aft to the officers' cuddy, where she apologised for her gear cluttering the place. He shrugged and briefly reverted to being her godfather, giving her a big wink and enquiring, "All well?"

"A bit tired and battered just now sir, it was a rough old trip. But yes, all well and the trip has been quite an experience."

"Fine. Let me know if you have any problems."

When the Admiral was delivered back to shore he took the boat's logbook with him and through channels they heard that the over enthusiastic Hurricane pilot who had shot them up had been severely disciplined. "I know what I'd have done with him" muttered Stan. After they parted, Jane found her quarters about half a mile away in the recently commandeered Dover College, a big Victorian building in its own grounds near the main railway station. There was a cool affability to the Quarters Officer's greeting. "Ah, Beacon, we've been expecting you. You'll be in cabin four along with some other killicks." She surveyed Jane's adapted bell-bottoms, "I hope you're not going to dress like that all the time? We expect our Wrens to look smart here."

"Well, ma'am, it's a practical rig for working on the boats, which is what I'll be doing. I do have proper tiddley uniform with me as well."

"That's just as well. We'll expect you to be properly dressed when you are not working on the boats, then. As a killick you will have to take your turn of duty here and to support the good running of the quarters, not that we have any problems. The girls are all as keen as mustard."

Jane smiled. "That's good to hear ma'am. I've not lived in a Wrennery before so it will be an interesting new experience." This caused Quarters Officer Braithwaite's eyebrows to go up, so Jane explained about life in HMS *Defiance,* her solitary rating status and her little cabin there and her life with the matelots on the mess decks. "Well, at least you'll understand our dear sailors better than my girls did when they arrived. Talk about some dodgy experiences. I think you will find things very different here, Beacon, but hopefully not unpleasant. The girls are a friendly lot although most are watch keepers so you only see them in passing. Will you manage in a Wrennery?"

"I don't see why not ma'am. After seven years in a girls' boarding school I imagine the atmosphere will be very similar."

"Oh, you were at boarding school? No homesickness, then?"

Jane smiled. "No, I got over that a long time ago."

"That's good. One other thing: our OiC (Officer in Charge) wants to see you at an early stage, so fix some clear time away from the boats sooner rather than later." And with that Jane got a nod of dismissal.

Letters were waiting for her. As well as the usual family missives there was a grumbly one in Punch's beautiful copperplate saying she was working as a messenger in the signals distribution office in Portsmouth. '*You'd think they could do something more useful with someone with my experience. They are talking about training Wrens as visual signallers and I might go for that, but please get us onto the boats soon.*' A cool one from Merle; she was going on the officer cadet course in May and expected to be third officer very soon. And an ecstatic one from Alicia, '*Jane, I've been accepted for despatch rider and should start in a couple of months. Oh, I am so pleased.*'

There was also a heavy official looking envelope of cream linen. Curious, Jane opened it to find a formal letter headed, 'Coutts and Co'. It confirmed that, on instructions from her father, an account had been opened in her name and ten pounds deposited in it. It gave details of her account and sort code numbers and how she could withdraw funds from it. There were also a cheque book and deposit book in her name. 'Thank you, father,' she thought to herself and that night sat down and wrote him a happy letter of thanks.

Having dumped her gear and read her letters, Jane looked round and was favourably impressed. The building's school origins were obvious, but its facilities seemed adequate and it was warm. Coming back to her new cabin she found a couple of other Leading Wrens in it, both communications specialists who had clearly been settled here for some time. She introduced herself and for the umpteenth time, explained what she was doing and why she was wearing bell-bottoms and a work blue shirt, rather than the skirt and white shirt that were regular uniform. Somehow, this seemed beyond the understanding of her cabin mates. "But Wrens don't go afloat, do they?" queried one. "Well, not officially yet. I'm very much an experiment, which is going fairly well so far, but I suspect the real test will be here, where I can be sent to any of their boats. Back in Guzz, I worked on the one boat and got to know her very well. Her crew were wonderfully helpful to me in finding my feet. Now, I have to perform with others who will be much less friendly to the idea."

Joanne, "But call me Jo" was a local from Dover with the characteristic pallor of the girls who worked underground. She proved to be a teleprinter operator in charge of a watch of girls and therefore liable to come and go at odd times. Jane noted this with a promise to be quiet. The other girl had a writer's badge on her sleeve too but somehow didn't introduce herself. A dark silent type, watchful and wary, leaving Jane wondering why. Jo chatted on, "The fourth girl here is Barbara, but she's on watch till this evening. Have you done any watchkeeping? It doesn't half mess your social life up."

Jane smiled. "Only at sea, but I've done a good bit of that by now."

"At sea? You lucky thing! I wish I could go to sea. I thought the Wrens would be the next best thing, but it's not the same somehow stuck down a tunnel."

"Oh well, we're hoping to see this experiment extended before long. There are a lot of matelots buzzing round harbours who could be out with the fleet."

"Do you really think girls can do it?" queried the silent one.

"Yes of course. You need physical toughness, but I'm sure we can find girls with that. There's certainly plenty of keenness."

A faint gonging echoed through the building. "Supper time. Do you want to eat?"

"Too right. Living in the fresh air and doing heavy physical work means I'm permanently starving. Lay on Macduff."

Coming into the mess hall Jane was struck by the noise; a tremendous blast of chatter and laughter and friendly teasing going on. How could twenty-odd girls make so much noise? But the cheerful happiness was palpable. Catering was self-service so she joined the queue behind her new cabin mates and collected her windy beans on toast. The silent one went off to join a small group tucked in a corner, so Jane followed Jo and found herself explaining yet again to Jo's watch what it was all about. The far away look on their faces told its own story. "Gosh, is that really a 'Mentioned in Despatches?" one of them asked, a bit big-eyed. "Oh yes," said Jane blithely and then had to explain how that had come about. She tried to play it down, but her questioner was sharp. "You were in the water almost half an hour in December? You must have nearly died of hypothermia."

"It was a bit cold, yes." Hero worship wasn't something she was used to. Although, the *Defiance* matelots had valued her in their own way, hero worship wasn't in their makeup. But here it was showing signs of growing up and Jane found it distinctly uncomfortable. "Can we call you Jane? We're told to be ever so respectful to our seniors."

"Yes of course. I'm not your boss, unless I'm on duty here and then it will take more than calling me Jane to stop you doing as I say. D'you know what a dreadnought is?" They looked rather blankly at each other.

"Well, let me tell you girls if you give me trouble you'll have one pulled over your head and your nose tweaked. So, if you want to risk it feel free to call me Jane." For days afterwards the matelots in the tunnels had difficulty keeping straight faces as their Wren counterparts pestered them to have 'dreadnoughts' explained to them. The idea of having one pulled over the head seemed to cause immense hilarity.

After supper, Jane sorted out a packed lunch with the Chief Wren in charge in the galley, explaining how she'd be on the water and not able to get to food otherwise, and arranged for an ultra-early breakfast. "It'll only be cereals and toast, help yourself to tea and we'll leave your lunch out." The lady replied. By now, Jane had form for getting round galley staff and set out to charm this one who proved very susceptible to a bit of flattery. 'Now for the boats of Dover,' she thought.

CHAPTER 3:
Onto the Boats

Refreshed and ready to go, Jane was at the boats office at 0629 the next morning to find a Chief Petty Officer opening up. She introduced herself and looked inside. Judging from the lists on the bulkheads there were neither many boats nor many boats' crew here. "The ships use their own boats a lot," explained the Chief, "but we need some shore-based ones for continuity." As well as *Amaryllis* Jane saw two motor cutters, a picket boat and something described as *Titch*. In addition, there were a large rowing cutter and two pulling whalers listed, but no work shown against them. "We make up the crew lists the night before," explained the Chief, "and they can see what they're doing the next morning and go straight to their boats. Mostly it's mail and stores runs and crew liberty boats sort of stuff. Are you familiar with that?"

"Oh yes, I can fish drunken sailors out of the dock" she said, getting a snort of amusement from the Chief in return. "Where am I on the lists?" The Chief pointed to the manning for one of the motor cutters. Under three names it said, 'The Invader'. "Well, that's not very nice, is it? Am I really seen so cruelly?"

"In some quarters yes. A lot of our crews will be off to sea if you succeed and they're less than keen on that. You've got a mountain to climb, Jenny."

Jane gulped. "I never thought it would be easy, but this sounds distinctly dodgy. At least I know what I'm doing on the boats, I think. Do we bother with things like boathook drill?"

"Only when you've got senior officers on board, or you're on a boat like *Amaryllis.*"

Other sailors were now appearing in the office, giving her long sideways looks and saying nothing. She took hold of the situation and asked, "Who is on the cutter *Sea Hawk?*" A long thin AB (Able Seaman) grunted, "Me", while a scrawny looking Stoker waved a hand vaguely. "All right, let's go." They both looked startled at this, almost an instruction, but trudged out behind her. The Cox'n, a three-badge Leading Seaman, was already on board and addressed them as a group. "Right you lot, let's get cleaning. Our first job is to pick up a squad from *Medway Queen* at 0730." Mops and buckets were produced from the stern locker and Jane started at the stern. Ten minutes into it, she turned round to find the others sitting there doing nothing, watching her. "Come on, you lot, get working. I'm not doing it all myself."

"Why not? Cleaning's women's' work."

"Come off it, not in this girl's Navy it isn't. Now get off your fat arses and scrub."

They looked startled at this. "Who are you to be throwing orders about?"

Jane pointed to the anchor on her sleeve. "See that? That's who I am to be giving orders. If you don't want orders from me don't try pulling stunts. Now get cracking."

The Cox'n nodded and said, "Come on boys, no more scrimshanking. Get going." And they did, to Jane's relief. None had bothered to introduce themselves so, when she had cleaned up to where the next matelot was working, she stowed her gear and went over to the Cox'n. "Hello," she said "I'm Jane Beacon. Nice to meet you." He nodded sourly. "Aye, ye might be right."

'Oh no,' she thought, 'not another Jock.' Then, he suddenly smiled and held out a hand. "Angus MacRoberts. We've heard about you, Jane. Are ye ony good or just a bit of a decoration?"

"I know my stuff, if that's what you are asking. I've been doing boats crew now for six months and it's gone well so far. There's only one way to find out if I'm any good here, isn't there? Let's give it a go."

"Aye, we'll do that lassie. Are ye ony good with engines?"

"Not really; I've been doing deck hand so far. Isn't that why we've got a Stoker?"

"Waste of a skin that one. Aren't you, Sharky?" Stoker Ward curled a lip.

"Come on, let's go. Jane, you take the bow." Sharky kicked the engine into life and they pushed out round the end of Prince of Wales pier and into the trots. *Medway Queen* proved to be one of the paddle steamer minesweepers, her elegant lines disguised by grey paint and a variety of extra bits tacked onto her. Jane hooked on forward automatically, busy looking at this strange new craft. An officer with wavy bands on his sleeve looked over the rails. "Come to get our lads, have you?"

Jane replied, "Yes sir, you have a group to come ashore for training?"

The officer jumped with surprise. "Good God, are you female?"

"Yes sir, I'm a Wren under testing for boat's crew."

"Well I'll be damned. What will they think of next? You must come aboard some time, have a drink with us."

"That's very kind sir, but now I've a job to do."

This conversation was interrupted by the training squad arriving at the brow, and filing onto the boat. Last in was a Sub-Lieutenant, also with the wavy braid on his arm. Jane had seen some of this during the run ashore in Newhaven so recognised it for 'hostilities only' reserve officers. Most of the ratings did not seem to be terribly pusser either. Once under way, the subbie wasted no time in speaking to Jane. "You're something new aren't you? Fancy a date sometime soon?"

Jane was unimpressed. "Not yet. I've only just arrived and the first person I speak to tries for a date. Bit forward, aren't you, sir?"

"I'll bet I'm not the last. But come aboard for a drink sometime."

"If I can arrange it I might." This conversation was cut short by them arriving at the steps, so Jane turned to her duties again.

In the course of a busy day three more people – a Lieutenant and two Petty Officers – tried for dates and there were any number of salacious suggestions, but by now Jane was well used to this and gave them relaxed humour. In one way this was so like Plymouth; lots of short runs moving people and stores around, continuous backchat from the sailors, but there was something different about it. These people were working right on the front line and underneath the banter there was a tension, which was new to her. This was brought home to her late in the watch when a fleet minesweeper came limping in under tow, with its stern missing. It had been blown off by a mine, which got caught in its gear. It berthed alongside and the injured and dead were taken off. *Sea Hawk* was despatched to lay alongside in case any boat movements were needed and their reliefs turned up for the late watch while they were waiting.

Jane found herself assigned to *Sea Hawk* for the next five days, and quickly she settled in to its routines. More slowly, the Cox'n moved from grudging tolerance to simply treating her as one of the crew, which Jane took for acceptance. Back at the Wrennery watch keepers came and went and it was four days before she met her other cabin mate. The silent one still hadn't introduced herself. With the initial surge settling down Jane began to think beyond doing her job properly. Jo seemed a good place to start, being local anyway. "Any good social life around here? For the moment I don't think I'll be working late watches."

"There's a lively dance on a Saturday night which swarms with Pusser's lower forms of life. My girls love it. It's not known as the 'grab and grope' for nothing. There's a couple of good out-of-town pubs, which are fun if you can organise the transport. Officers mostly drink on board so you need to get invited to their parties. There's usually a raft of invitations on our notice board. The best fun I think is the Chiefs' mess events. They know how to enjoy themselves without the toffee-nosed bit you sometimes get in the wardrooms. Plenty doing. Take your pick."

"What do you do yourself?"

"Me? I go with the Chiefs. But then I've got someone special there."

"Really? Anyone I know?"

"Probably not. He's the jaunty in one of the destroyers."

"Oh, right, I haven't got that far yet."

"The Chiefs are having a party this Saturday night and you could come along if you want?"

"Well, fine, that would be nice. Count me in. Uniform or mufti?"

"Oh, uniform I'm afraid. They are the Chief Petty Officers of the Royal Navy. Got a standard to keep." Jane simply smiled at this.

Saturday night found her in her smart new doeskin best uniform, tagging along with Jo to a local hostelry where the upstairs room had been taken over. Chief Petty Officers large and small, old and young, thronged. Jane spotted Stan in a corner quietly nursing his pint as always and went over to chat. There was something almost cosy about being with him again. Mild concern for her welfare was overlaid by obvious professional pride that he had brought her on so successfully. For his part he'd settled into the chief's mess very well, thank you, and *Amaryllis* was being kept busy without being over pressed. He'd heard on the galley wireless that reports about her so far were good and if she needed anything to let him know. As she got up to circulate she couldn't resist giving him a hug and a kiss on his bald patch from sheer affection and watched him go pink.

It struck her strongly that this group of solid citizens were the backbone of the Navy, the strength of character and self-confidence around the room almost physical in its force. And unlike the junior rates desperately looking for the next easy date, this lot had partners with them. Given that some of those partners were complete battleaxes they had to be wives and Jane was amused to see gimlet eyes being kept on husbands. She joined Jo and was introduced to her special. He in turn produced his chief tiffie and chief cook, both young and suddenly Jane found herself being appraised again. So, they weren't all married. Her Mentioned in Despatches oakleaf was spotted right away and once more she had to explain it all. At least this lot didn't seem to think it was an outrage that a mere female could get an award and they were politely respectful of her achievement. The invitation to their mess wasn't long in coming "*Venomous* on the second trot, but we're coming alongside on Monday to store. You could drop down and join us in the evening." Jane cocked an eyebrow at Jo, "Fancy that?"

"I'd be going anyway so yes, let's do it."

Jane smiled at the group. "Looks like you have a date."

She then drifted on and found herself with a group of Chief Wrens, middle-aged and well-upholstered women who were curious about her without showing much enthusiasm. Here, she was interrogated rather than taking part in a conversation, but their main concern seemed to be that her lurid disciplinary record had got here ahead of her, and they wanted to make it quite plain that she needn't behave that way with them, whatever 'that way' was because it was obvious they didn't know the details. Jane escaped their clutches as soon as she decently could and circulated. By now she was getting used to beer and happily nursed a pint as she went, having it topped up at intervals. As a result, she was in a relaxed state when she encountered a tall well-built young man with an obvious athleticism. The crossed clubs on his sleeve explained that. "Well hello, I'm the physical training instructor for Dover. I like working with the Wrens; so willing."

Jane gave him an unimpressed look. The double *entendre* was too basic to amuse. But that didn't seem to put him off and they chatted for some time about his problems in keeping fit the staff – male and female – in the tunnels. Then, his conversation got personal and Jane thought, 'here we go again'. The message seemed to be that he was the number one ladies' man in Dover, and was almost conferring a privilege on her by showing an interest. "You're a good looking bint," he said, getting closer to her, "fancy slipping out the back with me?"

Borrowing from naval habits, Jane looked him up and down coolly. "You must be joking. If you think you're getting me up against a wall in the back yard, then you don't know much about women. Do I look like that sort?"

"All girls are that sort when they fall for me and they all fall for me." He averred, apparently unaware of how crass he sounded. 'It must work with some of them' she thought, 'or he wouldn't do it'. He was certainly a striking physical specimen, handsome in a rather obvious way. She could see why unworldly girls could be taken in. But she wasn't one of them. Just to put him off she said, "Listen sunshine, to get anywhere with me you'd have to do a lot better; find a place where it can done in comfort and privacy. And not tonight."

'There,' she 'thought, that should put off a chancer like this one.' Jo and she had to hurry to get signed back in to the Wrennery in time. This was another new restriction to Jane who was beginning to realise how much freedom she had enjoyed in *Defiance*.

A day off was something to be treasured, a chance to catch up on personal matters and maybe get out a bit. In the morning, she did her dhobi, musing gently on how well Eustace had looked after her despite the price she paid in being spied on and how different her world was now. Then Barbara, the fourth inhabitant of her cabin whom Jane had hardly spoken to yet, remarked that she was going to church and would Jane like to come too? Religion had always rested fairly lightly on Jane's shoulders but the mores and theatre of the Anglican Church were deeply ingrained and suddenly it struck her that she hadn't been inside a church since Christmas. She enjoyed the familiar hymns and rituals and afterwards she felt good as they returned to the Wrennery catching the very last of dinner. There were few other girls about so Jane took the opportunity to quiz Barbara about their silent cabin mate.

"Oh, it's a sad story that. Even I don't know it all and I've shared with her for six months now. She's Jewish, y'know."

Jane shrugged her shoulders, "So?"

"Her extended family are mostly in Europe and she's permanently worried about them, as well as quietly being scared witless about what could happen to her if the Nazis invade."

"But surely she could be posted somewhere a bit further away from their arrival point?"

"She doesn't seem to want to; feels it's her duty to stay as close as she can to the action. You'll often see her down by the ferry pier when the boats come back from France; in case any of her family are among the refugees coming off."

"How sad. But why does that stop her talking to us? I don't even know her name."

"Esther – Esther Goldstein. She's a highly qualified physicist as well, apparently brilliant at some sort of research, which she doesn't make much use of in charge of a watch of teleprinter girls. No wonder she looks sad and far away."

"What a waste."

"Well, she's a volunteer so can't blame anyone else."

"Should I say anything to her? Offer a bit of friendship or anything? It's difficult to know what to do for the best."

"I don't think she wants help from anyone. She's very self-contained and doesn't seem to want friendship. The rest of the girls here are a very close-knit lot, but poor Esther simply goes on quietly in her own little world. But her watch rate her very highly; she's a tiger in looking after their interests."

Jane said nothing, but tucked the information away for future reference.

Monday morning at 0630 felt a bit grim, but she made it. Her assignment had been changed to the other motor cutter, No.P36, known locally as The Beast. Her crew were as unenthusiastic as the first lot had been, but Jane was learning to keep her head down and get on with the job as the best way of thawing out the opposition. Their first job was a mail run, then a pile of potatoes to be distributed round. Humping the sacks was on the limit of Jane's strength, but she would not admit defeat, working with the other two hands to get them out and onto the receiving decks. Then, they had to smarten up quickly to collect three destroyer captains for a conference ashore, before going round to the trawlers with boxes and boxes of ammunition. These were equally heavy and by the time they'd heaved them over trawler bulwarks her back ached. Collecting a group of trawler Skippers who seemed much more relaxed in their approach to naval protocol, they ran back to base and paused for lunch.

She had barely said a word beyond working comments, so introduced herself to the Cox'n, who turned out to be from only a couple of miles from her own home and knew of her father. This helped him to relax and they chatted while munching their sandwiches. Casually she asked him, "Why is this one known as The Beast?"

" 'Cos it's got Kitchen gear."

"Pardon? I don't see a sink?"

"No, my lovely, Kitchen gear is named after an old Victorian Admiral who invented it and it's how the boat is steered and controlled. Hadn't you noticed? She's not got a tiller, only a bar with a wheel on the end. There's no rudder, she steers by two bucket-like things, one each side of the propeller. They can rotate from ahead to astern and in intermediate positions direct the propeller's wash to one side or other to steer. The engine runs the one way all the time. When it works well it's brilliant but if it's not a good set it can be stiff and a complete pig to work with. Luckily this boat's got a good set. I believe you've done a good bit of boat handling already?"

Jane nodded enthusiastically.

"Fine, you can have a go after lunch. I'm bored with driving this bloody thing."

Which meant she spent an interesting afternoon getting the hang of the gear; quite tricky to begin with because it was a counter-intuitive new mindset to work it properly. But after a couple of frights she started to get it right and to see how manoeuvrable the boat was, able to stop in its own length and equally to turn right round in a boat's length, almost going sideways if required. And although she didn't know it, she got a glowing report on her boat handling abilities.

CHAPTER 4:
The Shadows Lengthen

"Happy birthday, Jane," was accompanied by her bed clothes being whipped off and having a large teddy bear plonked onto her semi-comatose form. This jerked her into full wakefulness on the spot. Bleary-eyed she tumbled out of her bunk. "Well thank you, but how did you know?"

"Lots of extra letters and parcels so we checked up; we can, y'know." Jo was obviously highly amused, as Jane yawned and stretched in the dawn light to be greeted by a chorus of Jo's watch singing, Happy Birthday to her from the doorway. "How old does that make you?"

"Twenty; just a year to go now."

The fourth of May was a big success. After opening her cards and parcels – there was even a pair of sheer black silk stockings from, of all unlikely people, her mother - she happily ambled down to the harbour to find The Beast's crew in on the act as well. They gave her another chorus of Happy Birthday as she came aboard and presented her with a big homemade card showing a seagull in Wren's uniform perched on the bow of a cutter spreading its wings while its droppings landed on the head of an Admiral. As a treat she was allowed to drive the boat all day and shout at the crew who thought it was a great wheeze. At tea in the evening there was a big birthday cake with the full twenty candles on it, which she blasted out in one lungful and she got a lot of fun from cutting it up and giving every Wren in the mess a piece. Apart from those on watch they were all there and even Esther The Silent, was seen to smile. She went to bed contented and full of happy thoughts about the girls she shared her quarters with. How kind they were.

But what the Navy gives with one hand, it takes with the other. From *The Beast*, cutter P36, she found herself assigned to *Titch*. This turned out to be a sixteen-foot clinker built skimmer of a boat with a little cuddy aft but otherwise open, only two of a crew and with a powerful marinised Morris car engine, which meant the boat went very fast indeed. Jane was used to rushing round in *Amaryllis* but somehow the same speed in this tiny boat was scary. Her Cox'n was a three-badge AB, a seasoned veteran of the proper Navy who greeted her with the usual naval stare. "I suppose you've come to take my job," was his surly greeting, which Jane could say little to because in all probability she had, hadn't she? But again her Cox'n thawed as he saw how well she was up to the job and for a few days all went well. On her fourth day on board she was bending over a pile of baggage, sorting it out ready for transfer when a hand suddenly grabbed and groped her between the legs. She whirled round and bang! The snake strike went in again, battering the old Cox'n against the boat's bulwark and nearly knocking him over the side. "You go sling your hook somewhere else," she snarled, standing over him as the boat careered wildly out of control. Quickly, she stopped the engine, pulled the Cox'n to his feet, looked him closely in the eye and warned, "Try that again and there will be serious trouble. D'you get my drift?" Nursing his face he straightened up, nodded silently and glared at her. For the rest of the day there was silence except for boat handling orders, which Jane was careful to carry out immediately and fully.

The next morning, she was dismayed to see she was not on the crew list, simply, 'Beacon report to Boats Officer' against her name. She smelt trouble from a mile off. Coming into the office she gave the officer her best salute and said sternly, "1095 Leading Wren Jane Beacon reporting, sir."

"Right Beacon, we've had a serious complaint about you. Yesterday, you refused orders and assaulted the Cox'n in charge of the boat you were serving on. What do you say to that?"

"He asked for it, sir and I did not refuse any orders."

"Asked for it? In what way?"

"If you must know he stuck a hand between my legs and tried some intimate groping. I won't have that and dissuaded him rather forcibly."

"Hmm, I was afraid of this. Women and matelots don't make a good mix. I really feel this so-called 'experiment' is going to have to be called off."

"What, you mean that I'm to be put out because one grubby old pervert stuck his hand up my jacksy? That's utterly unfair. I've been doing a good job and no-one else has had the slightest difficulty with my being female. You can't just call it off because of one incident."

"Don't you go going giving me orders, young lady. I'll decide what is to be done here. You can't claim special privileges because you're a Wren."

"But sir, I wasn't trying to claim special privileges. It wasn't me that made a complaint. I know our matelots quite well enough to know how to deal with them and I was perfectly content to deal with this business myself. I'll not be traduced in this way."

"You'll not be tra… what-ed?"

Jane grimaced in exasperation. "I'll not have it that it's me that should be in the rattle for this little incident, sir. He was not encouraged in any way. I did not disobey one order from him, and had done what was required of me completely and zealously. Should I lay a complaint against him? Would that help? I don't think so." The Boats Officer – a decent old passed-over two and a half ringer – growled in exasperation. "Well, young lady, I have a specific report on the table, which I can't ignore. I think I'll ask your Wren senior officer to help me with this. You are suspended, meantime." And she was dismissed from the presence.

Which is how Jane found herself summoned to see her First Officer rather sooner than she expected. This lady proved to be younger than the Wren senior officers Jane had met before and had a distinct Scots twang but different, more sing-song, than the way Fiona had spoken on the Probationer Course. Jane's records were spread out in front of her. Jane had come to attention, saluted and reported on coming into the office.

"At ease Beacon and sit down. I've been reading your records with the Director's comments all over them. You must be the only Wren rating she has taken so much trouble over. Talk about a one-girl storm. Why are you causing so much strife?"

"I wish I knew ma'am. Part of it is because I am the only one doing boat work and that's controversial in itself. In Devonport, I lived in an all male lower deck community and it seems I acquired all too many of their bad habits and attitudes from that. And part of it comes from naivety; the sexual bit was me getting a bit carried away."

"Yes, well that's obvious and I can't pretend I think much of your morals, but that's not really what concerns me in this instance. It's clear you are an intelligent and educated young woman; why are you a rating?"

"Ma'am you can thank the Navy for that. The WRNS is pursuing a belief that we can crew harbour boats perfectly well, I've been put in as the test pilot and I want so much for this to succeed. But in the Andrew all small craft crews are ratings and we seem to think we have to ape that. So, I'm stuck with being a rating. And anyway you have to be twenty-one to be an officer and I'm only twenty."

"And you like being on the boats?"

"Oh God, yes ma'am, I love it. It's doing a demanding, useful job which gives it purpose, but beyond that, out there on the water I really come alive. It's hard to describe unless you've experienced it, but being in the boats is a different world. There's magic in it; the dawn runs and the endless battle against the elements and the beauty of the sky at night when you're on the water. Sunsets look different there. It's a form of living close to nature; words can't describe it."

"You're not doing a bad job of getting the message over right now."

"Would you like to come out with us for a day? You'd love it, I'm sure. Shall I arrange it for you? Shouldn't be difficult."

Her First Officer shook her head in amusement and irritation. "Beacon, I'm in charge here and you don't go organising my life for me. If I want to spend a day with you on the boats I can arrange it for myself, thank you." Jane looked a little crestfallen.

"But don't worry, I think that's a very interesting idea and I'll see about following it up. Now, about this *contretemps* yesterday. Tell me about it again." Jane went through it, not that there was much to tell; a grope and a slap for it were hardly headline news.

"And you don't want to lay charges?"

"Not at all ma'am. I dealt with it in the way the lower deck understands and there it would have ended if this silly man hadn't put in a complaint against me for assault. Now, it's on the record and has to go through official channels, but I'm damned if I see why that should put a stop to the whole experiment. There's bound to be things like this when men and women are working in close proximity and there's no reason why they shouldn't be dealt with quickly and simply at the time unless they're very serious."

"For a young woman, you have a remarkable degree of understanding."

"Do I really? I'm not convinced I do, but so much of this is Jack's version of common sense. If you know your Navy the rest follows to my mind."

"Right; your precious Boats Officer is in a complete funk about this and has passed the buck to me. I'm afraid something will have to go on your somewhat colourful record, but I'll make it as mild as possible. If you don't feel any need to take it further I don't think I do either, but do be careful where you waggle your backside in future, won't you?"

Jane couldn't help laughing at this, stood up, came to attention and saluted. "I will, ma'am, I will." And four days later Jane had the pleasure of showing her First Officer what life on the boats was like. Despite it being a raw damp day, the lady left with her cheeks glowing and a much warmer understanding of what was at issue.

Next Jane found herself sent to 155, a splendid old picket boat with a brass bound bellmouth funnel, a coal-burning steamer with a beautiful little reciprocating engine. Jane was fascinated by its little open legs, bobbing up and down, and found it the warmest place on board. These boats had been the workhorses of the Navy, but by 1940 they were virtually at the end of their careers; old age and more efficient diesel technology overtaking them. The craft needed a crew of six and was used much more extensively for work outside the harbour breakwaters. She was a good sea boat, able to punch her way out into the Strait to liaise with convoys, to transfer orders, people and critical stores. It was as well that Jane did not suffer from seasickness as the gyrations were spectacular at times. Nor was it long before Rear-Admiral Rodmayne was a passenger, going out to meet a couple of major naval vessels passing through. A quick, "All well?" With raised eyebrow and a smiling nod in reply were all that was necessary between them. In a crew of six, Jane was less conspicuous, but she had to counter a degree of organised glimping, in the Naval sense, which took days to fade and was irritating while it lasted. Her uniform of bell-bottoms and Wren jacket over her lean frame would have been pretty androgynous had it not been for the obvious bulge of her generous bosom.

Six days after Jane's birthday, Germany invaded the Low Countries with a ferocious *blitzkrieg,* which sent the defensive armies reeling. Suddenly the atmosphere in Dover changed; the tension crackled in the air and everyone was showing the strain on their faces. The teleprinter girls were working flat out the whole time and Jane's cabin mates were coming off watch absolutely exhausted. There was a sense that after the phoney war period and the dismal effort in Norway, the real war had suddenly started.

Walking back to the Wrennery that day after having been well out to seaward chasing minesweepers with fresh orders, she was surprised to have the tall PTI drop alongside her. "Hello there. Care for a drink?"

Jane checked the famous waterproof watch. "I've got twenty minutes before I have to be back in quarters for tea. It will have to be quick."

They left wheeled into a local and he ordered two pints. Inevitably, they talked about the German invasion and what it might mean, but it wasn't long before he got to the point. "I took up your invitation and I've got a room organised for the night in a pub a little north of here, where we can be private. Which day would you like?" This rather took the wind out of Jane's sails. "You what? You've got a nerve. I don't even know your name, let alone have the slightest wish for you to touch me."

"I'm Eric, Eric Bates sometime known as Taff because I'm from the Rhondda, originally. Come on, there's a war on and you won't get many opportunities like this one." He said this in a teasing way, but clearly expected Jane to fall in with it.

"You really are the giddy limit. I've never met anyone so full of themselves. The best I'll do is meet you for a drink at this place, but no promises of anything more. I'd have to organise a sleeping-out pass anyway and those are pretty scarce. How can I get a message to you?"

"Leave a note at reception in *HMS Wasp* – that's the Lord Warden Hotel – and I'll pick it up." With that they parted, Jane hurrying off so as not to miss her tea.

Leading Wrens could have a little more latitude in their passes and Jane, bemused by her own stupidity, arranged an overnight pass for the following Saturday after having fixed Sunday as her day off.

Meantime she had a date with the wardroom of *Medway Queen.* They came alongside on the Thursday to store and load fresh sweeping gear and in the evening Jane popped down with Barbara to join them. They proved a cheerful bunch, a mix of the ship's peacetime crew called up for the duration and volunteer reserve types with no previous experience of the sea. The drinks were served by a large and florid

Lieutenant who introduced himself as Dylan. He had been a car salesman before the war and had lost none of his *bonhomie*. The regular crew were a shyer group, but thawed as the evening went on. Hovering over it was a sense of impending Armageddon and deep-seated worry about what was going to happen. But that didn't stop them being really friendly and it was clear Barbara was taking a shine to the first Lieutenant. Jane carefully restricted herself to being nice to them all, although conversation with the second engineer was a bit heavy as he explained the complexities and problems of the ship's boiler. But it was pleasant to be back in an officers' wardroom with its more civilised grace notes. An escort of half the wardroom saw them back to the Wrennery with thirty seconds to spare for signing in. Barbara looked quite dreamy as they hastily changed and abluted before pipe down.

The next few days on 155 were so busy Jane barely had a moment to think about her Saturday date, the ship running non-stop from 0700 until the change of watch at 1700, with their reliefs keeping going to the early hours. The fires were never drawn in her little boiler between washings-out and they were having to take coal every other day. This was a filthy process, which they all had to join in with; Jane shovelled with the best of them while being less than impressed by the state she got into. It was the first time since scraping *Amaryllis's* bottom that she had needed her boiler suit overalls. Over the horizon, the defending armies were collapsing and being driven back towards the coast of France and Belgium. The distant rumble of gunfire could be heard and for the first time German E-boats, (or S-boats, as they called them) appeared in the Straits along with forays by *Luftwaffe* Stukas.

But overshadowed though it was, social life went on and Saturday evening found Jane scrubbing desperately at her coal-grimed hair and skin, finding out that the bloody stuff got everywhere. She had sneaked six inches of bath water but even that was barely adequate for getting clean. After some debate she put on the black chiffon – how appropriate might that be? – and splashed some perfume about. Her PTI did a doubletake worthy of Jean-Pierre when he saw her, murmured, "Wow" and escorted her to the waiting taxi. The pub was ancient, scrubbed stone flags and polished wooden settles, mainly men in it but enough other women for Jane not to feel out of place although perhaps a little overdressed. They had a reasonable dinner in the snug and moved back to the saloon bar to chat with their drinks. Jane set out to find out a bit about this overweening man, and found her suspicions confirmed. Beneath the veneer of super-confidence he was a little boy, still pining for mum and the valleys. But he did radiate a powerful animal magnetism, which washed over her in waves as they talked and he pressed his thigh against hers with suggestive rubs.

By the time last orders was called she had given in, part of her rational brain protesting but the rest of her thinking 'what the hell, I've nothing to lose so might as well enjoy it while I can'. He had checked her virginal status and seemed relieved when she admitted to being beyond that. To her demands of what he did about contraception she was introduced to *coitus interuptus,* or getting out at Fratton, as the Navy calls it, which left her a little worried as being a bit too unreliable for comfort. The bedroom was ridiculous, a huge four-poster bed, heavy drapes, flock wallpaper and suggestive prints on the walls.

He undressed her slowly, savouring the moment. He came to her bottom and felt the ridged scar stripes across it. "Bloody Hell, what's that?" he asked.

"I got a caning on Probationer Course and it left permanent scarring. You can thank the Navy for those!" she said offhandedly. Clearly, he would have liked to know more, but she nipped into bed and pulled the covers up. He chucked off his own clothes and dived in beside her. Unfortunately, this was a warning of what was to come. Without so much as a warm-up kiss he climbed on top of her and banged away with great vigour for about ten minutes before withdrawing as promised at the critical moment. He lay there panting beside her.

"Is that it?" she enquired.

"Isn't that enough? Don't worry we'll do it again."

"Well, wow."

He gave her a funny look but obviously didn't understand the sarcasm. And do it again he did; another three times for successively longer periods, but each a repeat of the first time. On the third time, Jane was half asleep and was left with a sneaky suspicion that perhaps he hadn't fully withdrawn at climax, but was sufficiently dopey not to notice properly. The last time, he sawed away furiously for thirty minutes and generated some spark of pleasure in Jane, but after the treatment she had known before, this all seemed very primitive. He was certainly fit; to keep going ferociously for so long without a pause was quite a feat of stamina.

The next morning during breakfast he tried smooching her into a greater relationship. "You're the best girl I've ever been with," he said.

"Best in what way?" she enquired. "All I had to do was lie there and let it happen. Don't you know anything about pleasuring a woman?"

He looked puzzled by this. "Wasn't that the best sex you've ever had?" he asked, the incredulity plain in his voice.

"Not entirely, no. If you want to have anything more to do with me you'll have to let me teach you how to please the girl as well. There's more to it than being a receptacle for your enthusiasm."

His puzzled look deepened. "Come on, with the experience I've got there's nothing more for me to learn. Look you, I know what I'm doing." Abruptly, the Welsh in him was coming through strongly.

"No you don't. All you know is how to please yourself."

He shook his head irritably, paid the bill and they caught a bus back into Dover.

At dinner the girls, virgins all, were giving her little sideways looks, giggling behind their hands and obviously waiting for something. Eventually Jo broke the stalemate.

"How was he?" she enquired rather archly, clearly thinking this was something very daring.

"Very fit."

"Is that all?"

"Just about. Bloody useless otherwise, not the foggiest notion how to pleasure a girl."

Eyes were big round the table, clearly expecting a bit more revelation, but Jane had never been given to sharing her private life with the world at large and wasn't going to start now.

"Just a big sack of beef with lots of energy. No real understanding of a woman's needs at all. A rubber bag would do for him." And with that she got up to collect her figgy duff, the topic closed. Although she hadn't intended it, within twenty-four hours his reputation as the great lover was in shreds and perversely Jane's stock on the mess decks had risen with each retelling of her offhand comments. In the meantime, from his retelling, her status as a red-hot rocket, plus the scars on her backside had also become common currency on the mess decks, neither of which did her reputation there any harm either. But alone in her bunk that night she thought longingly of Jean-Pierre's ministrations and again it was dawning on her how special her time and experience in *Defiance* had been.

Inevitably, coming aboard 155 the next morning, there were comments and sly digs. "Show us your scars, love" was the least of them. But Jane, knowing from her days on *Defiance's* mess decks that trying to play prim and ignorant wouldn't wash, simply smiled gently and suggested they start with their own collections. And as had happened before, the matelots were more relaxed with her, more accepting of her as one of their own. Briefly, she toyed with the thought of doing more of it then Stan's words came echoing back in her head, 'Start putting it about and you'll be fair game for every canteen cowboy in the outfit and your life wouldn't be worth living' and as quickly as the thought came, she rejected it. Less would undoubtedly be more in these circumstances.

However, beyond her little orbit the world looked bleak. A week into the *blitzkreig* and already the German army had trampled Holland, charged through the Ardennes forests and were driving the tattered remnants of the defensive armies before them. A fresh draft of Wren communicators arrived to supplement the watches in the tunnels and it was clear the pressure on them was intense. As quickly as her cabin mates' interest in her doings had arisen it vanished in a miasma of exhaustion. In the harbour things were busier and more destroyers were arriving, but everyday routine continued. Jane was transferred back to *Amaryllis* suddenly, greeting Stan and Nobby for the old mates they were and within minutes she was back in the old routine. Much of it consisted of ferrying Admiral Rodmayne about, or bringing captains to him as the marine traffic grew more intense by the day. His little Admiral's flag board became pretty much a fixture on the bow. It would take more than a war on the doorstep to shake Naval routine, or so it seemed in those final few days before their world changed forever.

CHAPTER 5:
Decision Time

Meanwhile, by May 24ᵗʰ Admiral Ramsay in his lair in the cliffs under Dover Castle had completed his plans for Operation Dynamo, the lifting of the British Expeditionary force from Dunkirk. The Allied defences were collapsing rapidly, and with the encircling Wehrmacht drawing the noose ever tighter, the only hope for the defeated British Army was escape. From the start there were serious doubts about how many soldiers could be rescued. While this was going on the Navy lifted substantial numbers from Boulogne as a dress rehearsal for what was to come and the British garrison at Calais bravely fought on with orders to stay and fight with no prospect of rescue. On 26ᵗʰ May that garrison capitulated, having run out of ammunition, causing the loss of two crack infantry divisions and one of armour. But it held up the German army long enough for the defences round Dunkirk to be solidified.

However, this meant that many of the naval vessels to be used at Dunkirk had tired crews and well-worn armaments even before Operation Dynamo started. The constant dashing to and fro across the Straits was taking its toll on machinery, stores and bunkers well before the actual Dunkirk evacuation started seriously. When the order to commence Operation Dynamo was given on the evening of 26ᵗʰ May, more than 27,000 troops had already been evacuated. And the forward squadrons of the Luftwaffe had shifted close enough to be harassing the ships operating around the Straits. But more ships were being called up and the collecting of small boats, so essential to the beach rescue, had begun.

* * *

Back in Dover Harbour Jane now found herself assigned again to P36, the Kitchen gear cutter and all day they were hard at work collecting and delivering people, delivering stores and ammunition, taking messages and instructions. With the increasing numbers of ships in the port, alongside berths were at a premium and ships were being held on the trots. This meant in turn that the harbour-based boats were taking their share of mooring duties and led to Jane being introduced to the ancient naval art of buoy jumping. When ships moor to the large circular buoys universally used in naval trots one or two seamen have to get onto the buoy to shackle on or pass the mooring ropes through their large iron rings. This could be tricky, sometimes dangerous work, which involves acrobatic leaping about on the buoys. They were bare, usually rusty, exposed iron forms with no safety features and no footgrips on which there was a great deal of heavy heaving on the mooring ropes, and often stiff steel wires or anchor chains used to secure the ships. It was physically challenging work at the limit of Jane's strength. With the sea never more than a couple of feet away from an unstable platform the risk of a cold salty dunking was always close by.

Jane got her first wetting when the buoy she was on rotated suddenly and threw her off. Cold, wet and spluttering, she was unimpressed to be ordered straight back onto the buoy and even less impressed by the cheers and jeers from the destroyer's fo'cs'le head mooring party. It didn't take P36's Cox'n long to realise that Jane was a powerful swimmer and hence a prime candidate for the job. But like all these things, there was a way to doing it and after the first half dozen she started to get the hang of it. A parting messenger rope knocked her off for the second soaking from which she emerged bruised and cross, but she gritted her teeth, recognising that success with this would remove one more layer of 'girls can't manage' prejudice.

The chaos from across the water was bringing a mixed swarm of people into Dover, unloaded from warships and ferries alike. Support troops, injured front line soldiers and most noticeably a motley flow of civilians of many nationalities came flooding in. These refugees came in every shape and sort. There were obviously rich ones with ample luggage and money, the women in fur coats and the men with dark Homberg hats and polished shoes. Clearly they had not trekked long distances to get to England. Others arrived, dust-covered and in no more than the ragged clothes they stood up in, some with tales that they had walked halfway across Europe. There were lost little children, bewildered ancients and distraught mothers minus their offspring. But they all arrived with a desperate look to them and an overwhelming urge to get as far as possible from the rampaging German forces. Esther The Silent had several successes in finding stray elements of her extended family. Loading these unwieldy and exhausted groups into a boat for transport ashore taxed Jane's skills and patience to the limit, especially when they treated her like some minor skivvy and left a mess behind in the boat. "They should be bloody thankful, not treating us like serfs," she grumbled to her Cox'n, but he simply shrugged.

It was kept out of the news in Britain, but the parlous state of the British army was known well enough by the boat crews operating in Dover Harbour; the crews of the returning destroyers giving them a running commentary. Above all, their frustration was the lack of small craft to link between the beaches and the ships lying off as close as they dared to come. Dunkirk has twenty miles of beautiful sandy beach stretching away to the East, very popular with holiday makers before the war, but it slopes at the shallowest of angles which meant that some hundreds of yards from the tideline there was still only a fathom or so of water. The ships offshore used their own boats but most of these were rowing craft, which both limited the number of people they could carry and made them very slow. By May 28th this lack of small craft for transfers looked likely to choke off the evacuation effort and it was at this time that the call went out for as many small boats as possible to be sent to the beaches. Contrary to popular myth, most were manned by regular naval crews. Although there were outstanding examples of bravery by civilian crews, they were a minority of those working the beaches.

Britain might have been standing on the brink of invasion and defeat but life went on. After working at the most intense pressure all day on the 27th, Jane shambled back to her quarters, damp from another ducking and collapsed with a groan on her bunk. "Doesn't look good, does it?" she casually remarked to the ever-silent Esther, flaked out on the next bunk. The taut twitching of Esther's cheeks and mouth told Jane how much tension there was beneath the silence. "No, it doesn't. Do you really think they will come across the Channel?"

"Hard to tell, but right now what's to stop them? Our Army's beaten and running away. We'll be lucky to see many of those boys again. The ones coming off the ships now are completely shattered and couldn't fight again to save themselves let alone us."

"I know Jane, but what can we do? The whole world's falling apart and we sit here doing our little bit. There must be more we can do, but what? I've thought and thought about this and simply can't see a way out. Maybe my sister was right, clearing off to America."

By Esther's standards this was a major speech and Jane felt the enormous pressure she must be under to unbutton like this.

"It seems to me that all we can do is keep doing our bit, whatever that is. With Mr Churchill in charge now, perhaps we'll take a firmer stance with Hitler, although whether that will help is pretty doubtful the way things are going right now."

"You know I'm Jewish, don't you? Our prospects are utterly bleak if those beasts do invade. I've heard from my family in Germany what they're doing to us and frankly it terrifies me. I don't want to die in a corner at the hands of some pig of a Nazi. At least I'd like a fighting chance."

Much of this had not occurred to Jane. She had been so intensely pressurised with her own work that it crowded out wider-ranging thoughts. But she could see that for someone like Esther that collapsing world held a raw and immediate threat. Jane thought for a moment before replying. "Well, y'know, we've always been good at muddling through and refusing to give in so there has to be a chance we'll do it again. But if we lose our Army in France it won't look promising. Is this defeatism or realism? I wish I knew. All I do know is that we shouldn't let these worries stop us going on with our bit because it's all the little bits added together which will build something not even the Huns can beat. We've got to keep going. I don't suppose that's easy when you're worried sick about your future, but what else can we do?"

Esther smiled, a twitch of her mouth, which never quite reached her eyes. "I suppose you're right but it certainly isn't easy. No grand gestures for us; simply keep going. I sometimes think that some grand gesture would be easier than plodding on with the world falling about our ears."

By now tears were coursing silently down Esther's cheeks and Jane got up to give her a hug. Words from a wise woman came to her mind. *"Courage, ma brave"* she murmured, "We'll do it, you'll see."

Esther briefly and fiercely returned the hug then pulled away, nodding slowly as she did so. "Thanks Jane, I can only hope you're right. I wish I had your certainty."

"Certainty doesn't come into it: if you saw those boys coming off the ships you wouldn't feel at all certain. But we've nothing else."

This debate came to a halt as Jo burst into the cabin and collapsed on her bunk in turn. She wailed, "God, that was terrible. I've never known pressure like it. You'd think we were planning the whole damn war."

"Right now we are, dear heart. What's the mood like in the tunnels?"

"Tense, but determined I'd say. Come on, let's have some supper."

Strolling into the mess Jane was struck by the quiet, such a contrast to the usual racket. But one look at the girls' faces told why; they were pale and drawn, worry gnawing at their spirits and all energy gone. Mechanically, they went through the motions of eating, their eyes far away.

Her conversation with Esther had set Jane thinking. Simply reacting and doing what she was told didn't seem enough. A strong urge took hold of her to do more, to do something greater than being a deckhand on Dover's harbour boats. But what? She was in uniform, under orders and expected to keep her place. And always in the back of her mind was the sense that what she did could make a lot of difference to the prospects of Wrens becoming boats' crew more generally. But, But...what? There must be something. As she drifted off to sleep the fog of uncertainty seemed denser than ever and her fierce sense of wanting to do something grew the more frustrated for its lack of focus.

Another non-stop day on P36 saw her coming ashore utterly exhausted at the end of her watch. Having miraculously managed to stay dry she trailed into the boats office to see what was listed for the next day. By now she was on easy terms with the old Chief Petty Officer who ran the place and asked him "Anything up?"

"Too right there is. *Operation Dynamo* has started and we're going to be even busier."

"What's that?" she queried.

"We're going to take the Army off the beaches at Dunkirk and bring them home. All the ships we've got are being sent over there. Dynamo's the plan for doing it."

"Ooh, can I go? I speak fluent French."

"Don't think so Jane. Our orders are to keep at it here."

She shrugged her shoulders and trailed wearily back to the Wrennery. Esther was on watch, but Jo and Barbara were both flaked out on their bunks, utterly drained. At supper, the girls were again subdued, the tiredness of mental exhaustion showing from intense concentration for eight hours without a break. Contrasted with Jane's physical exhaustion, there was a debilitated edge to their lack of spark. The talk was cautious; most of the messages they had handled had been titled Secret or Top Secret but it was clear to Jane that something major was brewing.

The endless flow of ships now coming in were crammed with troops who had a fatigue to them that made Jane's tiredness seem trivial. In mid-afternoon the next day, her old friend the *Medway Queen* moored up and she greeted its people cheerily. "This job would be all right if only we could get more small boats to link between beach and ships." Dylan, the former car salesman told her. "We're desperately short of stuff to lift soldiers from the beach."

Jane noted this, wondering why none of the harbour's useful boats had been sent. Coming into the boats office at lunchtime she again raised the subject with the Chief, who referred her to the Boats Officer. Coming into his office she saluted smartly and asked, "Shouldn't we be sending some of our boats over to help? They're desperate for them."

The old officer shook his head sadly. "No Jane, we have clear orders to keep serving the ships here in Dover and surely you can see they're needed every bit as badly here."

"Yes, but they're needed even more badly over there." And she looked at him quizzically.

Thirty years in the Navy kicked in. "Beacon, we have orders; now obey them. There's plenty to do here."

Shaking her head in confusion she left the office, still feeling strongly that something more should be done. Yes, dammit, something would be done. It all came clear in her mind; she would take a boat across to the beaches and make some kind of contribution to lifting soldiers off, orders or no orders. To stay here simply wasn't good enough. It could only be P36 with its Kitchen gear, the others all needed a stoker to operate the engine and she would go alone. It would need fuel, some fresh water to drink, some lub oil, some grease for the gear, a compass and preferably some food. How long was she going for? She had no idea, although the talk was of two days. The boat would be running in Dover until midnight or so, so she would have to wait till then to take it.

With this decision the tension seemed to drain out of her and a clear way forward lay before her. She would do it; she would save soldiers and make a contribution. She would show those blinkered officers what could be done with a useful motor cutter.

"And that, Mrs Goodall, is how I decided to go to Dunkirk to see if I could help."

PART TWO:

RECOVERY

CHAPTER 6:
The Convalescent

The young VAD (Voluntary Aid Detachment) nurses formed what was virtually a guard of honour as Jane left the hospital and even Sister Donaldson relented with a warm smile, taking Jane's hands in her own. "Do take better care of yourself, Beacon. We need girls like you." And with that enigmatic comment she turned away.

Coming through *HMS Lynx's* lobby Jane saw Jo and gave her a cheerful wave from her stretcher. Jo came rushing across to her and went pale. "Dear God, Jane what's happened to your face?"

Jane shrugged. "Shrapnel, I think. They tell me it will get better as it heals and settles."

"Oh, that's terrible. I'll come up and see you this evening."

And from then on Jane had a stream of visitors. Jo came to apologise for her unthinking reaction in the lobby. Barbara came and prayed by her bedside. Esther came and sat in silent contemplation before bursting into tears. She gabbled, "If everyone's like you, those beasts can never come," and ran off. Next day Chief Officer Currie brought her impressive presence in, but there was a restraint to her concern. "You do realise you'll have to appear before a tribunal when you're well enough, don't you?"

Jane nodded sadly. Out there somewhere, beyond the concern for her welfare, a big black cloud was hovering, which she could dimly discern, but knew little about.

"I'm beginning to understand the Director's comments on your records. Are you still determined to stay a rating in the boats?"

"If that's the price of staying in the boats, then yes I am, ma'am."

"You could earn more as an officer elsewhere."

"Ma'am the money doesn't matter. I've quite enough to live on anyway."

"So, you have private means?"

"Well, support from my father, anyway. It does help."

"Which means we have to consider any future for you as a Wren rating." This was statement more than question, which left Jane to think about what that meant.

"Is there anything else you want at present?"

"Well, one thing perhaps ma'am. I really know very little about the Wrens. Is there anything I could read to get to know the service better?"

"Not a lot, it has to be said. I could lend you my copy of Dame Katherine Furse's book on the First World War Wrens and there's the WRNS regulations, which are pretty dry stuff. But not much more."

"Oh, even those would be helpful."

And next morning both were brought in by the Quarters Officer on her regular daily visit. Chief Officer Currie had been right; the regulations were very dry reading indeed, but Jane persevered and got to know rather more about the underlying structure of the service she had blithely signed up to.

At lunchtime the Lieutenant doctor called by with another copy of the *Times*. "I've managed to get myself appointed your regular daily check-up visitor."

"Oh that is good, sir. I shall look forward to that."

"Listen, now we're away from formality you can drop the sir. I'm called Jamie Macwhirter, so please call me Jamie."

"I'll be happy to, Jamie. With a name like that you must be Scots?"

"My parents are. Dad came from Scotland as a junior doctor and never quite went home again. We're from Hawick in the borders originally, but I was born in Kensington."

"What a co-incidence. My father's a Scots doctor from near Huntly. So, we have a fair bit in common."

"You're not medical yourself?"

"No, I had a place at Somerville to study French literature and philosophy, but that went by the board when the war came along."

"Ah yes, the war that you're winning singlehanded."

They looked into each other's eyes and laughed, a happy uproarious laugh of a sort Jane hadn't had for a long time. Somehow her afternoon was brighter. Later Mrs Goodall arrived; without actually seeming to do much she was drawing the festering horror out of Jane, letting her go on about the things she'd experienced and the regular sessions restored much of Jane's inner solidarity. But something remained heavy inside her, a knowledge that she didn't fully understand; a sense of being different now from other people.

During the next few days, Stan came by several times, awkwardly turning his cap in his hands as he stood by her bed. "Ee lass, you did it this time," was his opening salvo then he settled to bring her all the gossip and chat from the boats. Dickhead was back with them and limped up to see Jane, tongue-tied and awkward. Nobby proved much more voluble as usual, bringing news of Taff who had done some brave thing shutting watertight doors when his destroyer was mined. The *Medway Queen* lot came by, full of *bonhomie* and smuggled a little bottle of rum to her, which Jane really enjoyed. Their laughter and wild tales of repeated trips to the beaches left her cheered up, and feeling much more alive.

When she was transferred, she had enquired about her watch and was given it, battered and broken. She arranged to get it mended by a member of Jo's widespread clan and was delighted when it came back ticking steadily, if still a bit bent. Putting it on again somehow gave her a fresh surge of energy. Even her non-favourite one night stand the PTI called, but the blast of abuse he got from Jane for getting her pregnant left him shaken and troubled. He left a bunch of wild flowers, clearly picked from some hedgerow, which he had been going to present with a flourish, but in the end left limply lying there. Jane looked at them and was going to heave them out in a fit of rage, then smiled to herself. It wasn't their fault, after all, so she got a vase and arranged them with some care. Strange, she thought, how these little feminine pursuits can sometimes be so satisfying. By now she was fully mobile, up and about and dressed again, but still under close medical supervision. A VAD nurse was always on duty although Jane was the only patient and the Quarters Officer called in each morning, checking on progress. Jamie's daily visits were a regular tonic and she found herself really looking forward to them. He brought more books and kept the *Times* coming and soon the ten minute check-up lengthened into a half hour debate about the Navy and current events and what might be going to happen. Even a cheerful optimist like Jamie struggled to sound hopeful. "They're massing on the other side and if they come there's only the Navy to stop them. But by now you'll have read that wonderful quote by Admiral Vernon about Napoleon's plans to invade England:

"I do not say they cannot come, sir. I only say they cannot come by sea.'"

Jane laughed. "I hadn't thought of it like that but yes, there's a lot of truth in it, isn't there?"

"Well, the Navy would certainly make it difficult for them. But the *Wehrmacht* is brimming with confidence and it seems they believe they can do anything, so I wouldn't be surprised if they tried."

"What else is the Navy up to?"

"Well, we're still evacuating our pongoes from the west coast of France although that's almost finished. Did you know the Italians had declared war on us on June 10th? As a result most of the action seems to be in the Mediterranean these days."

"No, I didn't know about the Eyties. I wasn't terribly bright on June 10th. But that won't make much difference will it?"

"Well, it certainly stretches us a bit more and dear old Winston seems determined that we will remain a strong presence in the Meddi."

"We're always struggling somewhere, aren't we? But I don't suppose the Jerries will stay quiet round here for long though, will they?"

"I doubt it," and he trailed off into gloomy contemplation.

By now Jamie's visits were stretching to nearer an hour and he got a serious rocket from his boss for hanging about there for so long. But the visits were doing Jane a great deal of good and his intelligent conversation was a real tonic.

During the next few days, events flew by fast. The stitches came out from their various parts of her anatomy, the Surgeon Commander called to check the wounds and ensure that everything was healing properly and enquired about who would look after her when she went home. "Oh, my father will. He's a doctor."

"A doctor, eh? Would I know him?

"Well you might sir; he was in the Navy in the First War. He's Johnny Beacon."

The Surgeon Commander slapped fist into palm. "That's how I know your name. Old Johnny Beacon, eh? Well I'll be damned; you'll be in good hands there. Give him my very best regards. I was his houseman in Haslar after the First War. You know, we really can't have Johnny Beacon's girl thrown out of the Service. Just isn't good enough and I'm going to say so. Well, well." And he wandered off shaking his head in gentle amusement.

One thing was troubling her. As the hair grew in over her long scalp wound, it was coming in white. Given the deep auburn of the rest, it showed up strikingly. This thin streak changed her appearance even more than the scar on her face and left her in a quandary about what to do. Each person she asked had a different view. Leave it, as it was dramatically different, colour it to match the rest of her mane, even shave the scar to leave a furrow up her scalp to emphasise her war wound status. It grew in vigorously and while she was still debating, it formed into a thick and strong streak along her scalp.

Several long and enlightening sessions with Sister Donaldson left her wiser about her own systems. With a doctor and a nurse for parents Jane had been taught the basic anatomy at puberty and Jean-Pierre had advanced her education a good deal more, but a whole new level of knowledge was now imparted. She was provided with a couple of diaphragms. "But they won't stop you catching diseases, so you must be careful," was the warning with them.

Mrs Goodall continued to come each day but the sessions were shorter and less intense. Her report back was that Beacon was making a good recovery because something seemed to be boosting her morale. The Surgeon Commander smiled gently to himself on hearing that, having a strong suspicion what the something might be. He had never seen his young Lieutenant junior looking so cheerful, the tuneless whistle going with him wherever he went.

With the stitches out and Jane steady on her feet again, Jamie gave her clearance to go out if she wanted. This was accompanied by an invitation to go with him to the pictures. "There's one of those Bob Hope road movies on. A bit of nonsense really, but fun." Jane accepted with unseemly alacrity. They both laughed a lot and hands touched in the darkness; they were not withdrawn. They then had to rush a bit to get Jane back in time to sign in at the Wrennery and when he gently took her in his arms she didn't feel in the least like resisting except for "Mind my ribs!" They were not the only couple saying goodnight by the door. Going upstairs to the sick bay Jane felt happier than she had been for a long time, but was so puffed by the time she got there that she was appalled at how unfit she was.

On Saturday, while she was quietly absorbed in A T Mahan's *The Influence of Sea Power Upon History 1660 -1805* – a demanding but fascinating eye-opener of a book - a smart nurse in a grey uniform with a short scarlet cape appeared in the sick bay doorway. Jane took her for a duty nurse and carried on with her reading. "Hello Jane" the figure said. Something about the voice made Jane jump. She whirled round. "Louise! Well I never. What brought you here?" And they embraced, a slightly stiff movement but heartfelt enough.

"Well, I said I'd stay in touch and when I got back to Blighty I asked about you and heard you'd been badly injured. That face is certainly not nice, although I like the streak of white hair. I had a long weekend leave so I thought I'd drop down here to see you. How did it go after we left the beaches? You obviously had a hard time of it." And they fell to telling their stories. By now Jane was going out freely so they went into town and had dinner together. Once past the stiffness of her calling, Louise was a lively and very funny lady and there was much laughter during the evening, leaving Jane feeling greatly invigorated if sore in the ribs. One thing was settled. Louise encouraged Jane to leave her white streak as it was and it became a distinctive mark for her throughout her Wren career. There was only one bad side to it; try as she might to insist on being Jane, inevitably she was christened Badger and from them on was commonly referred to as Badger Beacon.

CHAPTER 7

Tribunal

Jamie's visits were becoming less and less professional and several times significant coughs from the duty nurse were all that stopped them getting up close and personal. Despite that they also did a lot of talking, discussing the books he was bringing her and debating naval policy and prospects. After ten days of this peaceful interlude Chief Officer Currie called again.

"Well, Beacon, you appear to be well on the way to full recovery. You've been warned that you will have to appear before a tribunal to answer the disciplinary charges laid against you. I think you know what they are?"

Jane nodded. "Yes ma'am. I don't intend to deny them but to plead mitigating circumstances."

"Mitigating circumstances? Have you become a lawyer or something? You've obviously not lost any of your wits, at least. Now, when you leave here you will go on convalescent leave until you are passed fit by the doctor in Plymouth. You can either appear before the tribunal before you go on leave, or it can wait until you're passed fit. Which would you prefer?"

"Oh, I'd rather get it over with and done with, then I can try to plan for whatever future I might have. I really don't want it hanging over me."

Chief Officer nodded. "I can understand that. You're sure you are up to it? If so, I'm going to arrange it for next Monday at Chatham. It will be a swords and medals occasion so be sure to have your best uniform on and be ready to come under full discipline again."

Chief Officer Currie's visit had brought into close-up the black cloud, which had been hovering in the background and she thought about it at some length.

"Jamie, what do you think I should do?"

"Oh, smile at them Jane and they'll melt in front of you."

"Stop it you idiot. This is serious. I don't want to be thrown out, so I've got to be convincing."

"Jane, your record speaks for itself. You don't need to defend yourself. All you have to do is tell them what you achieved and they are bound to forgive you some minor naval transgressions."

"But they're not minor, Jamie. Disobeying orders is enough in itself to get me dismissed, never mind going absent without leave and what I did to P36."

"Yes, I went and had a look at it. They've craned it out and it's sitting on the quay. It's amazing that it kept going in such a battered condition. But then you and it are a pair. Really, Jane, you have nothing to be scared of."

"Oh, I'm not scared, only worried because I want to go on serving on the boats. That is my life."

"Come here," and despite a significant cough from the nurse they had a kiss and cuddle, which cut short any further debate.

By Monday, Jane had bribed a Wren steward to press her best doeskin uniform, polish her shoes and generally ensure she looked as smart as possible. She even put on the silk stockings her mother had sent for her birthday. She carefully arranged her white lanyard round her neck tucked under her jacket collar, drew it tight across her chest and stowed her clasp knife into the jacket's inside pocket. None of this was strictly Wren ratings' uniform but Jane was past caring; looking smart seemed more important. For the first time, she pinned on the bronze brooch version of her Mentioned in Despatches oakleaf over the sewn ribbon and topped it all off with her battered uniform hat – burnt round the edges - a hole in the front where the shrapnel had cut into her scalp and a grease mark on the back where she had used it to wipe down the Dorman engine. Transport had been arranged for her for 0830 and it turned out to be an Austin Ruby just like her mother's. By 1100 she was in an anteroom waiting to be summoned into the tribunal's presence, rehearsing in her mind her arguments for doing what she had done and what it had all achieved. A friendly Petty Officer Wren had greeted her and seemed to be in charge outside the tribunal chamber, shepherding Jane along.

Entering the chamber, Jane was struck dumb. Behind a long table were a Captain RN, a secretary Lieutenant-Commander and a young but studious looking Lieutenant. On the Captain's other side was a Wren First Officer and her own OiC, Chief Officer Currie. A large pile of papers lay in front of the Captain. A single seat was placed opposite the Captain; it looked very lonely. 'All this for one errant rating?' thought Jane, 'wow'.

At one side, stood a small but fierce Regulating Chief Petty Officer. "Leading Wren Beacon, step forward. Halt. Salute. Off hat. Report yourself."

She stepped up to the table, came to attention, saluted, pulled off her hat and reported, "1095 Leading Wren Jane Beacon, sir".

"Thank you Beacon, please sit down. I have here with me Lieutenant-Commander Jones as secretary to this hearing. He will be taking the official record. Then there is Lieutenant Davenport. He is a qualified solicitor and will advise us on any points of law which arise. On my left is First Officer Lady Cholmondley from Wren headquarters. Chief Officer Currie I think you know.

You are here today to answer serious charges laid against you.

First, that on two occasions you disobeyed direct orders given to you by a Royal Naval Officer.

Second, that you went Absent Without Official Leave for eight days.

Third, that you took Admiralty property, namely launch P36, without permission and misused it, returning it in a seriously damaged condition.

In addition, it is the official view that the beaches of Dunkirk were no place for a woman and you should not have been there. What do you say to these charges?"

"I can only plead guilty, sir. It is plainly evident that I did those things. I can only plead mitigation that I did it all for a good reason. They were desperately short of small boats on the beaches and I was able to make a significant contribution to rescuing the Army."

"Yes, yes, we know all that, but it does not take away the charges. The Navy takes a very dim view of such obdurate behaviour and the normal punishment would be dismissal from the Service. Did you know that when you went? "

"Not in so many words sir, but I knew it was without official sanction and there were liable to be consequences. To be honest, I didn't think much about that at all, sir. All I knew was that there was a desperate need close by and I could help do something about it, so off I went."

"Yes, quite so. This tribunal has to decide what to do for the best as good order and discipline have to be upheld and be seen to be upheld no matter how good the intentions might be. Which means that we have to decide your fate according to a much wider set of conditions."

There was silence for a minute while this was digested. Jane had been about to speak again when the Captain held up a hand, looked at her and said, "Are you aware that the Army, as well as the French are pushing for you to be given medals and made a heroine? The Army want you to join their ranks in the ATS?"

Jane shook her head. "No Sir, I am not."

And she looked at them enquiringly.

The young lawyer cut in. "So, when you went, it was not with visions of glory and fame?"

This was getting ridiculous. "No sir, it was not. I'm afraid I don't know what you are talking about."

"Oh come, come Miss Beacon. This was death or glory stuff. You went through the flames and the bombs and it was not to win glory?"

The red mist was welling up inside her, sweeping aside the carefully planned debating positions.

"No, it was not. I went to save as many of our boys as I could and I don't give damn whether you approve of it or not. I did it, I did it." And to her intense annoyance she burst into tears, banging the table in front of her. "I did not do it to win medals or glory or any other fancy bits. There are three thousand four hundred and twenty-seven people who survived because of me. That's something I know I did and you can't take that away from me. Stick me in detention or dismiss me if you must." And a mixture of pain in her ribs and incoherent fury left her slumped, sobbing and grinding her hands on the table. Gasping against the pain, she pulled herself upright and glared at them through her tears, defying them to do their worst. There was a prolonged silence on the other side. This sudden eruption of raw emotion had left them wrong-footed, leaving them feeling awkward and puzzled and uncertain what to say.

Eventually Lady Cholmondley broke the silence. "All right, Beacon, we understand. Our problem is that you have admitted to committing three serious offences against discipline and regulations. The circumstances are unusual but we can't ignore the offences. Can you say anything else?"

Taking a grip of herself Jane replied, "Well, P36 was the ideal boat for the job and if we'd had more like it we could probably have saved even more people. We left a lot of French behind, y'know. To that extent, I feel I did the right thing, with or without official sanction."

"Huh," grunted the Captain.

Jane continued, "I know orders were put out for me to return but towards the end they were glad to have the boat and me to do some difficult things. And it was only the Navy that had any problems with me being there; the Army seemed delighted. This bit about the Army wanting me in the ATS is new to me, but it says something about my usefulness. But having survived over there I'm kind of numb now; there's nothing more can be done to harm me. I very much want to stay in the boats and to go on showing what girls can do, but apart from that nothing seems so important any more. Do your worst. I'm past caring."

After this speech, the group looked at each other and the silence lengthened again. "Miss Beacon, I think we need to discuss this. Please leave us for now."

Jane nodded, came to attention and left. The friendly Petty Officer Wren who had met her was waiting. "Like a cup of tea?" she enquired.

"Oh, yes please, I'm dry as anything."

Jane was sitting quietly sipping her tea when she was called back. "Don't dump it, I'll be back for the rest."

The Captain spoke. "Miss Beacon, we have considered what to do for the best here. We cannot have regulations flouted as you have done, but we do see that there were good intentions in what you did. We have received a series of glowing written depositions from interested parties and read the medical reports as well as the Report of Proceedings from Lieutenant-Commander Lord Daubeny-Fowkes. It is clear that you did some splendidly brave and useful things on the beaches. Against that Commander Leslie does not seem to have been impressed by you and his report is less than complimentary."

"What! He could not have been more enthusiastic over there. How could he say things against me? Although I was wounded and the boat in a mess he gave me difficult jobs to do and was full of thanks at the time. I don't believe this. The two-faced scumbag."

The two Wren officers winced.

"Miss Beacon! You will not refer to any naval officer in those terms. Apologise and retract that now."

Jane raised her eyes and sighed. "All right."

The Captain glared at her. "If you don't want to demolish what little chance you have of surviving this, you will refrain from comments like that."

"Yes sir," she said flatly.

Her mind was in turmoil, thinking 'How could he double cross me like that?' But the proceedings rolled on.

The Captain put his cap on and spoke again. "Despite your little outburst, we have decided to admonish you and warn you not to act against good order and discipline again. We will stick with that decision. I am advised that the Wrens are keen to keep you despite your errant behaviour and I take full note of that. We will not disrate you this time, but if you can't take orders you're not fit to give them. Go on like this and you will find yourself an ordinary Wren again or worse very quickly. On the other hand we feel that some recognition of your bravery is called for; but what that is will be decided by the medals committee. But there will be no publicity and no making a public heroine of you. We cannot allow it to become known that ratings can defy their orders and get away with it. Whatever is decided will be done very quietly. In the meantime, you can go on convalescent leave and once you are passed fit for service again please contact the WRNS headquarters. You have been warned before not to contravene the regulations and we repeat that today; one more disobeying of direct orders and you will be dismissed, no matter how special the circumstances. All this will go on your already lurid record. Is that clear?"

Jane could only nod. Somewhere, somehow, a guardian angel was keeping a wary eye on her. The little Regulator barked "Leading Wren Beacon, attention. On hat. Salute. Left turn, quick march." And Jane quick marched out of the chamber to her cup of half cold tea.

Back in Dover, she went to the boats office for the first time since going to Dunkirk and got a very friendly welcome. Although the Boats Officer kept out of the way, the rest were waiting for her and by a sneaky arrangement to celebrate her joss she got gulpers all round. Could there be any finer demonstration of lower deck approval? Probably not, but it was a powerful one and she tottered back to the sick bay in a thoroughly unsteady condition. Before she left, there was a small presentation; a white ensign and a steel helmet with RN on it. The flag was ragged and burnt round its edges and had half a dozen holes in it. The white was grey with gunpowder and the filth of war. It was the ensign she had flown on P36 throughout her time at Dunkirk. "We thought you might like it as a little souvenir." Turning in, dreamily she draped it over the head of her bunk, picked up its hem and kissed it, smelling the gun smoke. For the first time since they started she had a sound night's sleep untroubled by her nightmares. When Jamie called round later in the evening to congratulate her, he found Jane unconscious on her bed and stinking of rum. He smiled, had a word with the nurse – now only on duty at night – and asked her to keep a sharp eye on the drunken body.

CHAPTER 8:
Troughs and Peaks

Jane was up and about early next morning, thick of head but otherwise feeling remarkably sprightly, when two large military policemen were ushered in by a nervous looking Quarters Officer. They took off their red caps and sat down, so it wasn't Jane that was in trouble. 'Makes a nice change' she thought to herself.

"Miss Beacon, we've come to ask you a few questions about some soldiers you picked up from Dunkirk. You brought three back to Dover with you. What can you tell us about them?"

Jane explained about finding them clinging to a navigation buoy in nothing but their underpants and that they'd told her how they tried to build a raft to get back to England.

"Was there anything odd about their behaviour and what happened when you got back to Dover?"

"Well, they huddled together in the bow of the boat and kept to themselves, but by then I'd seen all sorts of strange behaviour from shell-shocked pongoes, so didn't think much of it. And yes, when we got in to Dover they disappeared quietly without saying anything. I was talking to the French officers and noticed that suddenly the three weren't there any more. Why are you interested in them?"

"We believe they are deserters who had tried to bribe a French fisherman to take them to England secretly. But it seems he robbed and stripped them then dumped them in the sea off this buoy you describe and sailed away. They're probably very lucky to be alive, but they won't think that when we catch up with them. If we make up a statement of what you said will you sign it for us, please?"

"Yes, of course provided it sticks to the plain unvarnished story."

They smiled grimly at this and nodded. An hour later, with the aid of mugs of tea, the statement was complete and Jane signed it after reading it through carefully. The whole business left a slightly sour taste, unsettling Jane for the rest of the day. It occurred to her that the two police officers probably knew a lot more than they had let on.

At lunchtime, Jamie called in and made a date for them to go out for dinner that night. Without a nurse on duty they could be more personal and it took a surprisingly long time for a short call to finish. Disentangling themselves, Jamie grinned at her, "Got to go, but see you at seven looking your best."

Jane smiled at that and said, "I'll do my best but nature's against me now, isn't it?"

"Jane, you look terrific to me anyway."

Encouraged, she looked out the black chiffon and arranged for it to be sponged and pressed. Dealing with her mane, now creeping over her collar despite Wren regulations, was a bit of a challenge and she had to rake back in her memory to the beautician's instructions about applying make-up, but by seven she was looking as good as she could manage.

It certainly worked for Jamie. "My God, Jane, you're gorgeous. I knew you were a looker, but this is something else. I'm honoured to be with you."

"Oh come on Jamie, don't overdo it. It's a pleasure to make the effort for you."

He smiled and offered his arm, as they set off to one of Dover's best restaurants, The Crypt, popular with service personnel. In his best uniform Jamie looked pretty smart as well. During dinner she looked at him closely; fair curly hair, the build of the rugby player he admitted to being and happy blue eyes. Although he didn't stand out in the crowd there was nothing not to like about him, thought Jane, and lots to approve of. But even he couldn't get past Wren regulations so they had to part at the door on time. Lying in her single bunk, this inconvenience set Jane thinking. She knew her time in the sick bay was up and she would be going home on convalescent leave within a day or two. Next morning she quietly arranged a sleeping-out pass, getting a very fishy look from the Quarters Officer in doing so.

Jamie arrived at lunchtime with a half-day off and a great deal of enthusiasm. In the quiet of the sick bay they got quite intimate and clothes rather dishevelled. Pulling apart, he looked at her as she tidied up a bit and said, "Jane, I think I love you. I've never met anyone like you before. Do you think you could love me too?"

"Jamie, I might well and to show it I've arranged something special. I've got a sleeping-out pass and tonight I'm going to show you how much I might love you too."

Jamie gasped. "Jane, that's wonderful. What are we going to do about it?"

"Well, I know of a pub north of here where we can have a room for the night."

Jamie pulled away and looked at her quizzically. "How do you know about a pub like that?"

"Oh, I found out about it."

"All right, but let me get this straight. You're inviting me to spend the night with you in a pub you know about. Am I to deflower you or something?" This said with a tone of wonder as he moved away from her.

"No, Jamie you wouldn't be doing that," and she held out her arms to him.

"You what? You mean you're not a virgin?"

She couldn't lie. "I'm afraid not, Jamie."

"Jane, how could you deceive me like that? There I was, thinking you were this beautiful pure thing like I'd never seen before and all the time you weren't at all.

What are you, some sort of whore trying to entrap me?"

"Oh, don't be ridiculous, Jamie. I've only had one other lover. And I've not deceived you, the question hasn't come up before and if you'd asked me instead of weaving fantasies in your mind, I'd have told you. Deception it isn't."

She was dismayed to see him collapse into tears. "Jane, Jane, how could you. I loved you so much and now it's all gone. I'm sorry, I can't be doing with used goods."

"What do you mean, used goods? Am I a bit of old clothing or something? I don't understand this at all. I am still the same person you were keen on ten minutes ago."

"But you're not, Jane, you're not." And he stood up, lower lip trembling and tears pouring down his face. "This is the end. I hope you recover well, but don't expect me to help you. Goodbye."

"Hah!" I had no idea you were such a prude. I'm beginning to think I've had a lucky escape after all. Goodbye then, Jamie."

And with that he rushed out of the room leaving Jane furious, but totally stunned. From cautious declaration of love to the end had taken a little less than half an hour. She sat there in silence, her brain more or less blank for some time. Slowly it dawned on her how much had just been lost; then the tears came. When the night duty nurse came on, she found her patient lying on her bed crying and sobbing. The nurse, a middle-aged woman, looked at Jane appraisingly and asked, "Men?"

Jane could only nod.

"Not worth it if you ask me. Don't let the so-and-so get you down. You're worth much more than that."

"Well thanks, but I was really starting to care for him and now it's all gone."

"There there, dear. You'll get over it. I have twice now."

"Yes but..." and somehow Jane couldn't articulate any more.

She had a bad night with the nightmares coming back with Jamie's face mixed up with the others, all coming to get her in some weird way and the night nurse had to comfort her several times. By morning her face was puffy from crying, but during her porridge, for the first time in a long time, the thought suddenly dropped into her mind, 'I will not be defeated'. When the Quarters Officer came in to see her at 1030 Jane was composed again.

"Right Beacon. There's a car going to Plymouth tomorrow taking two senior officers. We're planning to put you in the front of that so you can have an undisturbed trip. Your roommates have packed your stuff so be ready to travel tomorrow morning at 0800. And good luck." Somehow her survival within the Wrens had passed, accepted as fact without comment and she was back in the system.

There was one more caller before she left. Rear-Admiral Rodmayne had phoned and at midday sharp, picked Jane up and swept her off to lunch. Once settled at the table he smiled at her. "I had no idea I was encouraging quite such a wild risk taker. Were you always like this?"

Jane shook her head vehemently. "No, sir, I was entirely well behaved and respectable at school. Leadown was quite a liberal establishment though, and we had a fair bit of personal latitude so I suppose the question never arose. I've been surprised by it all, too."

He laughed gently. "Be honest with me, why did you really go to Dunkirk? It was such a crazy thing to do."

"Uncle George, may I?" He nodded. "Uncle George, it really was simply as I said at the tribunal. Have you seen the record of it?" Again he nodded. "I felt it was quite wrong for all those useful boats to be doing no more than buzzing round Dover harbour when there was such a desperate need only forty miles away. Really, I went because it was the only way to get a boat there then one thing sort of led to another...." And she trailed away, looking into the distance, then started up again. "It really wasn't bravado on my part, I only went to do my bit."

"Doing your bit has caused a great many complications, as I'm sure you know by now. The Service has to be able to rely on people doing what they're told. I know we encourage a degree of thinking and initiative, but it's pretty circumscribed and certainly not to defy direct orders. You're a very lucky young lady still to be in the Wrens y'know?"

She nodded, looking sad. "Well, I'll try to be more obedient. I don't actually disobey orders that much, but I seem to make a spectacular job of it when I do."

Suddenly he smiled. "But from what I've read you were incredibly brave on the beaches. I always knew you had a strong character but not on that scale. As an Admiral I'm not allowed to say it but if you promise not to say a word to anyone I'll tell you that I think you have done a marvellous job. I'm so proud of you Jane but because of your disobedience, I can't say so publicly."

Jane smiled. It was a lop-sided smile now, constrained by the still healing wound on her left cheek and saddened by a knowledge inside her that she was only slowly coming to terms with. Softly, dreamily, she said, "Just think, if it hadn't been for this war I'd be up at Somerville now, studying French literature and drinking sherry. Instead, I've developed a taste for beer, I'm all bashed up, seen lots of dead men and horrible wounds, big bangs and crazy aeroplanes shooting at me and some pretty vile behaviour by desperate men. I'll never be a blushing virgin bride now and all that in nine months. How long do you think this silly war will go on for?"

"Who knows? One thing's for sure; it will not be over by Christmas. But Churchill arriving at the top has changed a lot of things, not least our attitude to the Hun. I have a suspicion that we may be in a for a long haul, but it will be a long haul with bursts of activity then longish quiet periods while we snarl at each other. But I'm quite certain the Navy will be busy the whole time, getting convoys through if nothing else. Assuming you want to, I think we may need your services for a long time yet."

This thought made Jane change tack. "Are we any closer to getting Wrens onto harbour craft, more generally?"

Uncle George pulled a face, "Hard to tell. There's still entrenched opposition but less so and the manpower situation is getting so bad that I suspect we'll have to use women a lot more simply to meet our commitments. If you keep going as you are, we'll be able to demolish some of the arguments about ability, but as for being good obedient ratings, that's another story. You always were impulsive, but this is a whole new planet."

Jane laughed. "I'm sorry, Uncle George, I really don't try to be difficult, but it sort of happens."

During this relaxed discussion a three-ring Wren officer had been eyeing them frostily from another table. At last she couldn't contain herself any longer and marched across to them, breathing heavily and red of face.

"Sir, I really must protest at your taking out one of our young Wren ratings. This is the sort of thing that totally undermines our efforts at developing a strictly disciplined and well-behaved service."

The Rear-Admiral looked her up and down in that very naval way. "My dear lady, I quite understand your problem and clearly regulations must be upheld. But if I chose to take my goddaughter out to lunch I will do so and you can be quite confident that it will not undermine good order in the Wrens."

The officer, a short stocky woman with a deeply lined but strong face, took a deep breath, clearly unsure about what to do next. "In that case, sir, I apologise but it remains a concern to me."

The Rear-Admiral smiled, "Please join us for coffee. Do you know Leading Wren Beacon?"

The lady's eyes opened wide in surprise. "Leading Wren Beacon? You're the amazing one who went to Dunkirk and caused us a lot of trouble? Well, I never." And the lady sat down with a bump. "I never expected to meet you, Miss Beacon. Did you really do all the things that the stories suggest?"

It was clear that despite the efforts to keep Jane's exploits quiet, there was an underground circulation of tales going round about her. So, Jane's answer was guarded, "Well, some of them, Ma'am, but I suspect they're being exaggerated already."

By now they were on the coffee, chatting about the Wrens' position in the service and whether Jane's activities affected that. Abruptly, Uncle George looked at his watch, said "Good heavens, I'm late," called for the bill, gave polite farewells to the Wren officer and ushered Jane out. "Give my regards to your parents and get well soon. We need you."

CHAPTER 9:
Persuasion

At 0755 the next morning she was dressed, breakfasted and ready to go. Esther and Barbara delivered her kitbag and suitcase fully packed, with her large teddy bear lashed to the outside of the kitbag. They packed her kit away in the boot of the car, which proved to be a large Rolls Royce saloon of uncertain vintage but great comfort. Having seen her stuff into the boot she climbed in to the front seat beside the Wren driver who was waiting patiently. She was about to say, "Good morning," politely, but instead it was, "Alicia! Good Heavens. But all that's wonderful, what on earth are you doing here?"

"Hello Jane. I'm still a Wren driver. I'm based up at Chatham but when I heard we were taking you as well, I fixed it with the driving pool to do this job. This is my last one before I go off for despatch rider training and I'm really looking forward to that. But it's great to see you. Now tell me, are the tales about you true? Your face has certainly taken a beating." There was a glass partition between front and back seats, so as they went round, collected the Admirals and set off for the West, they were able to chat and gossip freely.

"And how is your bottom now? That must be another set of scars."

"Oh, scarred enough and not a pretty sight any more, but it works and I move freely so I suppose I'd have to say, not too bad, thank you."

"Did you hear about dear First Officer Brown?"

"No, what happened? Do tell."

"Well, the story goes that once we'd all gone and the furore had died down she was summoned to headquarters, given the most ferocious bottle imaginable, told that brutality like that had no place in the Wrens and was sacked. She tried appealing to the law that she had acted legally but the judge hearing the case has a daughter in the Wrens and was appalled by what he was hearing. Case dismissed. Now I believe she's an officer in the ATS."

"They're welcome to her. I had quite enough to cope with without plotting revenge but if I ever meet her again I'll wring her neck. When the Director interviewed me it was obvious she wasn't impressed and I felt then that I was getting a fair hearing. Well, well." And Jane snorted with amusement.

By lunchtime they had passed Southampton and the Admirals were hungry. Jane and Alicia had both brought sandwiches, but their passengers expected something grander, so Alicia took the car into the middle of Bournemouth and stopped at the

Royal Bath Hotel on the waterfront. The girls had been going to sit on a bench looking out to sea to eat their sandwiches but the Admirals had other ideas. "Would you two ladies like to join us for lunch?"

Wren The Honourable Alicia Stewart D'Aincourt asked, "Do you really think we should, sir? We're only junior ratings." Her cut glass accent rather negated this, but the protocols were fairly strictly laid down. "I think for once we'll overlook that. In any case we want to hear about Beacon's adventures."

The two were swept into the dining room with the Admirals and enjoyed a very high standard of service. Jane told them about her exploits and the explosion, which had injured her and what it was like on the beaches because they were both desk Admirals. She skirted round the tribunal and the charges laid against her. "It is amazing that a girl can do something like that," remarked Admiral one.

"Yes," ventured the other, "these modern women seem to get up to all sorts, don't they?"

Jane saw this as an opportunity. "Well, you know, sir, we are actually capable of doing a lot more than we've been asked to do so far. I know it's not considered right by the older generation, but we young women are very willing to do so much more. You know I've been crewing on the harbour boats since the start?"

No, they didn't and some time was spent exploring that and how Jane managed with the lower deck. "No problem, sir, they've almost entirely been very good to me. I'm sure you know they have their own code and once you understand that it's not difficult to get along with them. There's some not keen on us Wrens moving in because it means giving up their cushy little billets but the rest are fine." She showed the Admirals her watch and for a couple of minutes they explored the relative value of this against being Mentioned in Despatches. On balance the watch won.

"You've successfully crewed on a harbour boat? How interesting. Where was that?"

"Plymouth at first sir, then Dover. I'm now going home on convalescent leave, but I'm expecting to go back to the boats at Dover when I'm passed fit again."

Admiral one looked at her intensely from under his bushy eyebrows. "War is very much a man's business and somehow what you're doing doesn't seem like the caring nurturing we'd expect from women. Are you really saying that you're willing to give that up to join the services and fight?"

Jane controlled her irritation. "Well sir, we don't actually fight; the idea is that we take over the jobs ashore that release matelots to go and do the fighting. We're young enough that the caring and nurturing can wait. Right now there are more important things to think about, like there's a war on and if we don't all pitch in we're going to lose it. I certainly don't want to see the Hun coming over here and beating us. They're gathering in France right now and could come any day so if we girls stick to our posts then perhaps our men will be that bit freer to defend us. But I suppose I could pick up a gun if they do come."

"Well, I never. Are you really as patriotic as that?"

"I'm not sure it's patriotism in that jingoistic sense, sir. I love this country and I've seen enough of Jerry now to know that it would be a horrid place if he took over. That seems worth fighting for. We've all been called to do our bit and mostly the girls I've worked with simply see it as that; doing their bit through to the end and hoping that makes a contribution, however small."

Admiral one turned to Admiral two, "Y'know Charlie, this might be the answer to some of our manning problems. I'd never thought of using women. I wonder if they really could do more demanding jobs?"

Jane couldn't resist butting in. "I'm living proof that we can, sir, and I know lots of other Wrens keen and able to do much more challenging things."

"You're a persuasive advocate young lady. I think we'll look into this. Do your senior ranks know about you?"

"Oh yes, sir. You'll find I am fairly well known at the top of the Wren hierarchy and I could suggest a few other Admirals who believe in us."

'Please don't speak to Gribben' Jane thought to herself, 'or we're sunk.'

"Charlie, I think we'll have to look into this, but now it's time to go."

They were now behind schedule so Alicia – a competitive hill climb driver before the war - pushed the old Roller to rather higher speeds and conversation was limited as she had to concentrate. But they bowled into Plymouth dockyard at 1830, dropped their VIPs at Admiralty House and retired for a quick drink. "Do you really think we've done some good there?" queried Jane.

Alicia nodded vigorously. "I'm sure you have, Jane. They took the bait completely. As they said, you really are very persuasive."

"That's easy when you've got a good case. When will you be fully fledged as a despatch rider?"

"I've got my motorcycle license already so only a couple of weeks, I think. I have been sounded out for officer but I've actually rather enjoyed the driving. You get about all over the place and there's lots of variety, up to three-ton lorries. Despatch riding should be even more fun, so I'm in no rush to get commissioned."

Coming into the hotel Jane had phoned her father at work. He turned up as Alicia was waxing enthusiastic about driving, took one look at Jane and cried out, "Good Goad a'michty girl. That's terrible." He could still turn very Scots when upset. She bought him a whisky and soda to calm him down and explained again about her injuries. A farewell hug with Alicia and she was on her way back home to the Grange, for the first time since she had left Plymouth on *Amaryllis*. That seemed like another world.

PART THREE:

HOME FIRES BURNING

CHAPTER 10:
The Haunting Past

Coming into the yard at the Grange was as close to pulling on a comfort blanket as Jane knew. Through the open kitchen window she saw her mother with cook, busy preparing the evening meal. Full of enthusiasm, she ran into the kitchen to give her mother the big warm hug she always got. But as she approached, her mother went white, wailed, "Oh, no," and sat down with a thump on the hardwood kitchen chair.

"Mummy, Mummy, what's wrong?"

"Oh Jane, Jane, you were so beautiful and look at you now," and she sobbed helplessly. Jane put her arms round her distraught mother, perhaps the first time that she had been the comforter, the leader in the emotional drama. "Mummy, it's not so bad. I'm still the same Jane and the medical people tell me this will get a lot better when the rawness fades away."

"Yes, but Jane, but Jane...." Somehow she couldn't articulate any more.

All this left Jane a bit puzzled. Earlier that day Alicia, the Admirals, even the hotel serving staff had been cool about her appearance, so why the drama now?

"What's wrong mummy?"

"Oh Jane, oh Jane, now you'll never get a husband."

"Oh don't be stupid. Finding a husband's the last thing on my mind. There's a war on, hadn't you noticed?"

"Yes, but...." Her mother trailed off into incoherent sobs. Her father, watching this from the doorway, said, "Let her be, Jane. I don't think you realise how much of a shock your appearance can be at present. I know it will calm down but other people may not. Don't make it too hard for her."

Jane stood up, shrugged and giving Eunice a hug wandered across to the range, peering into pots and sniffing with enthusiasm. "I'm starving even after a good solid lunch. Can we eat soon?"

Her father raised his eyebrows but said nothing and half an hour later they were sitting round the dinner table with her mother more composed.

"When are you going away again, dear?"

"Why, are you trying to get rid of me already?"

"No, no, no. That's not what I mean and you know it. How long have we got you for?"

"That depends on how well I heal, but the doctors at Dover seemed to think

I needed a month off. My ribs are pretty sore between times and I think that'll be the deciding factor. When are the kids due home?"

There was a moment's silence before her father asked, "Kids? What are kids? Is this some terrible new slang term?"

Jane looked startled. "Yes father, I think it came from the States but I hear it often enough."

"Well, I'm not sure I am keen on it round here. I presume you mean your younger brothers and sister?"

"Yes, of course."

"I suppose we have to move with the times, but I can't say I like it."

All Jane could do was shrug. Her parents had never heard Jane refer to her younger siblings as being children different from her and there was a brutal if quiet shock in realising how much she had matured in a short time.

Her mother replied. "The twins are due home about the end of the week. David's gone sailing for a couple of weeks with one of his school chums and Sarah's off to ballet school for a week, but they should all be home before you go. I do hope you can see them all and Granny Beacon and Aunt Bidgie are arriving together next Tuesday."

"Oh, that will be nice," said Jane a little uncertainly. Her younger brothers and sister were so much part of the fabric of life that she had never thought of them as anything special. But her Granny and especially Aunt Bidgie would be nice to see again. Her father's younger sister was an elegant spinster who lived in a flat in the New Town in Edinburgh and had an important job as a manager in one of the department stores on Princes Street. To Jane, she had seemed the epitome of female sophistication and had always been someone to look up to.

Her mother spoke again, in a quiet sad voice. "This war really is tearing everything apart, isn't it? Already we're losing you and David's going to Dartmouth in September and now Sarah's talking about leaving school as soon as she can to join the Wrens, and.... and.... I don't know. I didn't bring up a family simply to lose them all to Herr Hitler's evil plans. What are we going to do?" This last sentence was more of a wail than question.

"You're not really losing me, mummy. This is my home and you're my parents. Keep battling, mummy, keep battling. You mustn't give up hope so easily. We're still here and we are well and still a family and that's what really counts."

Her mother could only shake her head slowly before turning her attention to serving the pudding. Through this her father had sat quietly at the head of the table, looking far away and grim. Jane knew vaguely that he had seen some tough times in the first war but he never spoke about them. She saw some long buried pain showing on his round friendly face. "My brother," he began and trailed off. "My brother.... Oh never mind," and his mouth turned down.

"Johnny, don't make it hard for yourself. It was all a long time ago." And suddenly her mother was stronger again, the helpmate and rock. "Shall we take coffee in the lounge?"

It was strange, but comforting to lie in her childhood bed again, the little spring below her hip poking her thigh as it always had done. 'One of these days', she thought to herself, 'I'll have a huge double bed with the comfiest mattress that money can buy.' And thinking vaguely of such luxury she drifted off into a dream of an angry Jamie and accusing faces coming at her through flashes and bangs as she lay spread-eagled helplessly on a giant mattress. But she slept well and next morning was up sharp at 0630 as usual. There was no-one around so she made herself a cup of strong tea and went back to bed. Next she knew it was 0845, the tea was cold and the household was on the move. 'Perhaps a lie-in could be excused as part of the healing process', she thought with an inward grin.

Her father was off to work early and the day gently drifted, her mother pottering in the garden, cook and the maid bustling about their routines and the postman's cup of tea a cheerful interruption. During the morning Jane prowled restlessly, finding the aimlessness difficult. There was something wrong about the place. Where were the outdoor servants? During lunch she quizzed her mother. "Well dear, young Tom signed up for the Army in April and Pappa Gianni has been interned."

"What? How could they intern Pappa Gianni? That harmless old man; he's been here for twenty years and they surely can't think he is a threat?"

"The day after Italy declared war on us, Churchill issued an order to 'collar the lot' and every Italian in Britain has been rounded up. We don't know what has happened to him and poor old Agnes is utterly distraught." Agnes was a local girl who had married the handsome Italian soon after the end of the First War and both had settled as servants at the Old Grange. Pappa Gianni was another part of Jane's childhood and life, as gardener and mechanic and general handyman to the establishment. The childless couple had doted on the Beacon children who in turn loved nothing better than sitting in Pappa's shed listening to tales about sunny Italy.

"But what could he possibly have done? He hated politics and Mussolini and was far too old to do anything against us. To take him away like this is pure cruelty."

"Your father protested, but the orders came from a very high level so we had to comply. He's still trying to see if we can get Pappa Gianni released."

Jane shook her head in sad perplexity. What had seemed a straightforward battle between good and evil had taken a very nasty turn for the worse. But after a lunchtime soup almost as good as the long-remembered *Defiance* sickbay bowlful, she lay down on the faded chintz settee and came to with a start at five o'clock. A cup of tea seemed like a good idea but she looked at the pale brown mixture cook handed her with some dismay. "God's teeth Eunice, this is real gnat's piss," she muttered. "Can't we stoke it up a bit?"

"Afraid not, Miss Jane, we've rationing now and to make the tea last we have to have it a bit weaker."

"Bloody war. It looks like being harder on civilians than the services at this rate. At least we still get a decent brew in the mess."

Dinner was a silent affair, her father wrapped in contemplation and her mother looking tearful. Jane was starting to long for her siblings to turn up if only to liven the place up a bit. During coffee her father suddenly burst into life. "I'll need to look at your wounds tomorrow, Jane. Remember I'm also your doctor for now."

"Oh fine, when shall I make an appointment?" The irony went over his head. "After breakfast. I've taken a half day off for this."

Next morning, she went into his study and stripped to the waist. He poked and prodded in her ribs producing the odd wince, scrutinised her facial scars with a magnifying glass then pulled off the dressing from the hole in her shoulder. This had been kept open to allow it to heal from the inside out and was still a little way from completion. Her mother, watching with worry all over her face, took over to dress it again. "Well, young lady...."

Why did they all talk to her like that?

"Well, your ribs are almost healed and your face is more or less fully mended. It's the hole in your shoulder I'm concerned about. The letter you brought says they cut out some material that was turning gangrenous and it is taking time for new to grow in. I expect it will, but probably not for a few weeks yet. That will be the deciding factor. Meantime, we have to let it heal from the inside outwards and dress it daily. I see you've been having bad nightmares as well, but the psychiatrist thinks you're getting over them now. Fortunately, I've been getting regular medical reports since you returned to Blighty."

"Yes, it's been the faces, the faces, they were horrible," and again she started to get worked up as she thought of them.

"All right, calm down, when you're ready you can tell us about them, but preferably not at the dinner table."

While in his study Jane had been looking round this holy of holies, barred to the children until 14 years old and then only allowed in to talk to their father. It was book lined and Jane noted many of them were on naval topics. "Father, I've been doing a lot of reading about the Navy while convalescing. Would you mind if I borrowed books from here to read?"

"Feel free, my dear. Use this room if you like; it will stop the children from pestering you."

This was a real honour. She spent a happy half hour browsing the shelves, decided against a heavy tome on health in Nelson's Navy and settled to read about the Battle of Jutland in detail. She knew her father had been at it and at least one of his medals came from that, but had no idea which ship he had been in. The book was heavily annotated in the margins. 'Not true!' against a description of a ship, which had seemed a bit lost. 'That was Jerome Hawkins' doing' against another description of a particularly brave dash by a destroyer. Clearly, her father had been acutely aware of what went on during the battle.

'I wonder if I can get him to talk about it' mused Jane, 'I'd know more about what he went through'.

At lunchtime she heard a strange keening noise coming from the kitchen. Puzzled, she strolled in to find Agnes utterly prostrate and emitting a surreal banshee wail with an equally distraught Eunice trying to comfort her. Her mother was sitting by the kitchen table, also in tears. "What on earth is going on here?"

Her mother looked up and held up a telegram. "Pappa Gianni was put on a ship to be deported to Canada. It was torpedoed yesterday and he was drowned. This really is beyond cruelty."

"Oh no, that can't be right." And try as she might to stand brave, Jane dissolved into tears too, sitting down beside her mother and trying to cuddle her. The afternoon was lost as they tried to pick up the pieces but Agnes was beyond consoling. Eunice packed her off to bed and when Doctor Beacon came home in the evening he unlocked the medicine chest he kept tucked away in his study, took out two pills and gave them to Agnes, trying to find a few words of consolation as he did so, but even his doctor's bedside manner could do little to comfort her. At least the pills sent her off to sleep.

Jane had prepared a series of questions about Jutland and the Navy ready for her father when he came in. With Agnes settled down Jane had launched them on her father who dealt with them good-naturedly, but without giving much away. After dinner Jane went back to the study to carry on reading but was only a page further on when her father came in. Again, she tried to get him to talk about Jutland and what he did to earn what she discovered was his Distinguished Service Cross, but he was reticent, simply saying, "We had to work in difficult conditions after the wardroom was hit by a shell. Fortunately, only a small shell but still enough to do a good deal of damage. In those days the wardroom was used as a casualty clearing station during actions. It's ironic, isn't it? I got some broken ribs at Jutland but like you managed to keep going." Jane smiled in fellow feeling.

"One thing I've never understood, father. From what I've heard you had a good career ahead of you in the Navy yet you left abruptly in 1921. Why was that?"

Her father gave Jane a sideways glance then stared long into the logs burning in the grate. In a low growling voice he said, "I suppose you'll need to know some day and perhaps you've acquired enough maturity now to handle it. It wasn't me that caused my departure, but my brother Archie. He was a Major in the Black Watch and had been in the trenches for more than three years when he was involved in the second battle of the Somme. He'd won the Military Cross and bar by then, so he was no coward. He led a hundred men over the top but they were decimated by machine gun fire and shelling and he only had about ten left by the time they retreated. He was also severely shell-shocked himself and from all accounts had more or less lost his mind. Despite this, he was ordered to lead his men in another charge right away and when he refused he was arrested for cowardice. He was summarily tried and condemned two days later. I only found about this in 1921 from the padre who attended him; we'd been told he was killed in action. According to the padre his mind had gone with no idea what was going on and he was a shaking weeping wreck when they tied him to the post. A staff officer who'd never been near the fighting slapped him across the face in contempt at his condition then they shot him. I was so angry about it that I resigned my commission the next week. Have you never noticed how against militarism I am nowadays?"

Jane, totally stunned, could only nod. She had never seen her father, that quiet, self-sufficient and slightly austere figure, like this and she saw underneath, a vulnerability never visible on his public face. The silence lengthened between them as her father stared into the fire, his jaw muscles twitching and his amiable round face contorted into something grimly savage. Eventually, Jane spoke, in a quiet whisper of a voice. "Was there much of that in the last war?"

He nodded. "A total of 306 people were shot like that; mostly other ranks, but a few officers as well."

"I always knew you had a thing about violence but never knew why until now. But you loved the Navy?"

"I did indeed Jane. But something broke inside me when I heard how Archie had died and I simply couldn't stand the whole military mindset for another minute. Watching you get involved in the same way, coming back to us scarred and roughened up is more painful than you can guess. I thought a girl going into the Wrens would be out of the line of fire, but obviously I was wrong."

Jane gave a wry smile. "In general you would be right. Uncle George gave me a real bottle about not being so impulsive, but I can't help it."

But that night the nightmares came back with the faces tied to posts and being shot at, screaming abuse at her. She woke up howling to find her mother holding her while her father looked on. It took some time to calm her down. "I thought I was getting over these," she said plaintively, when the heaving sobs had subsided. For an hour she raved about the faces and the added pain of hearing about her uncle before she finally slumped and drifted off to sleep again. Her worried parents kept vigil in turns for the rest of the night, but she slept on through whimpers and groans.

CHAPTER 11:
Family Connections

Her father always brought the day's *Times* home with him so it was evening before any news could be read and for Jane it was the following morning before she opened the paper and looked at yesterday's news.

* * *

"French fleet destroyed at Oran," shrieked the headline. *The report went on to detail how the British Navy had shelled and destroyed a substantial French fleet tied up in the port of Mersa-el-Kabir, Oran. This sad action was a reflection of the confused politics of the moment. With France overwhelmed and signing an armistice agreement with Germany, the French fleet became a major pawn. Britain was concerned – terrified might not be to strong a word – that this large and powerful Navy would fall into German hands because this would totally change the balance of power at sea. It would give Germany the sea strength to be able to mount an invasion of Britain and to paralyse its sea trade routes. At the same time, French politics were cloudy and ever-changing and it was impossible to get clear understandings of the French position. Therefore, the French fleet was given the choice by Britain of immobilisation in places where it could do no harm, of coming over and joining the British in fighting on, or being sunk by the British. No such undertakings were received from France and individual Admirals had to make their own choices.*

At Mersa el Kabir, Oran, in North Africa lay the substantial French Mediterranean fleet. Outside was the British Mediterranean fleet, augmented by HMS Hood and other lighter warships. These two fleets had been sailing together as close allies a few weeks before. All through July 3rd tense negotiations went on to get this fleet to surrender, steam out and join the British, or immobilise itself, but no undertaking could be obtained. Therefore, acting under direct orders from Winston Churchill, the fleet under Admiral Somerville opened fire at 1800 and destroyed all but one of the major ships lying in the port. The Battleship Strasbourg escaped to Toulon in Vichy France. Admiral Somerville, in command on the spot, described it as the most distasteful thing he had to do in his entire Naval career. This, along with actions elsewhere against other elements of the French fleet, sent severe shockwaves through France and it is no surprise that French Naval personnel turned overwhelmingly against their erstwhile allies. This made life very difficult for the French people of all sorts who had come to Britain to continue the fight against Hitler because they were now being seen as traitors by their own people back home. Many soldiers and sailors who had stayed on in Britain after Dunkirk elected to go home in disgust and the whole episode cast a long shadow over Anglo-French relations. But it did take the French fleet out of the reckoning and the feeling at a political level was that, on balance, this was more important than keeping the defeated French friendly towards Britain.

* * *

The Silent Service kept its counsel and did what it was told. Like all Francophiles Jane was appalled by this action. The eldest Pechot boy was a midshipman somewhere in the French fleet; he had been a brother to Jane ever since she started coming to them six summers before. And where was Jean-Pierre? She had heard nothing from him since the Portsmouth visit but presumably he must be with the fleet somewhere. She could only hope they would be all right.

She railed at her mother and Eunice. "How could they do this? It's criminal." But those ladies could only shrug their shoulders. After a frustrating day of marching up and down steaming with rage Jane ranted at her father when he came home. He looked at her in that very naval way but, well accustomed to her explosive moods, took it calmly. "Well, you've certainly not lost any of your spirit, that's for sure. War is a messy business Jane and the damage can be widespread. I don't suppose you've thought much about what you are doing, getting involved in it?"

"But I'm doing my bit. We all need to for the sake of the country, don't we?"

"That's all very well my dear, but the particular bit you're doing can turn from a patriotic duty to mindless destruction very easily. War is a cruel and brutal affair, which wrecks much more than it achieves and by doing your bit you are contributing to that destruction."

"Oh, come on father, what are you, a conscientious objector?"

"No, my dear I am not and I actually agree that we have to defend ourselves. But you mustn't fool yourself into thinking it is a great or glorious business. What have you read about it so far?"

"Oh, various history books about the Navy and Nelson and now about Jutland. It all seemed like strong patriotic stuff."

"Can I suggest some alternative reading, here on my shelves? Try this anthology of First World War poetry, especially Wilfred Owen and try the *Iliad*; have you read that?"

"No, I haven't. I did modern languages at school, not classics."

"There are good English translations. Here, look at this one." And he pulled a thick tome down from a high shelf. "I think you'll be surprised by how anti-war it is."

Jane looked doubting but took the books. "What am I supposed to get from these?"

"Alternative viewpoints and something to make you think. Please don't feel that I'm trying to put you off doing your bit, but it's best to do so with your eyes open."

The call to dinner interrupted this conversation but Jane found herself thoughtful through the meal and retired early clutching the books. She tried a few of Owen's poems and the English student in her found them delightful pieces of language but she struggled with the sentiments. The first stanza of the Iliad sent her off into a deep sleep, which she emerged from at midnight, dumped her clothes and crawled under the blankets.

She woke early the next morning and picked up the poems again, finding it hard to get inside them. Then, she turned to '*Dulce Et Decorum Est*' and it hit her hard. The gassed soldier; that was Eunice's brother. The middle two lines with the face coming at the writer; that was her at Dunkirk.

"In all my dreams, before my helpless sight,
He plunges at me, guttering, choking, drowning."

How could he possibly have known about the drowned soldier under the boat, or the French Lieutenant's head, or the mad staring eyes of the young Captain who had shot holes in the boat? But there it was and suddenly these dry poems from another era came alive to her. Her Latin was good enough to translate the ending and to see it called a lie, that was hard. That was the uncle she'd never known. "Oh father, why did you give me this?" she whispered to herself. Jane was glad when her mother came in with early morning tea and dragged her out of her waking nightmare.

"Why so sad, Jane?"

"Oh, these silly poems father gave me to read. They're scary."

"That's your father for you. I learnt a long time ago not to go into his darker recesses. Why do you think I stick to home and family?"

"I thought that was because you loved us and saw it as your job."

"Hah! You won't know how good a ward sister I was. I love your father dearly, but I have always had a sense of vocation missed. As for his precious poetry, I know it, but I find it easier not to think about those sorts of things. Cowardly perhaps, but I do find it too much."

This left Jane deeply confused. Was her mother not happy with her family and home? Was there something else she yearned for? Or were these peaceful, contented surroundings an escape, a way of hiding from some more brutal, more painful reality? All these puzzles made for an unsettled day. She tried more of the *Iliad* and sort of saw what her father was getting at, but all these Gods interfering with mere mortals and the endless recounting of bloodlines did not make for stirring reading. The laments of the Trojan women struck a chord, but she also had a sense of irritation at their feebleness.

Which meant that by dinnertime she was more than a little out of sorts. Her mother tried some brisk conversation.

"The twins are due home tomorrow. I've managed to scrape together enough petrol to meet them. Do you want to come too?"

"I suppose so, better than hanging about here and it would be nice to see Plymouth again."

"Don't you want to see your little brothers?"

"Well yes, of course, but what's so special about them?" Jane was puzzled that there should be any sense of event about young siblings coming home from school.

Her mother shook her head, looking perplexed in turn. "With this dreadful war on I have a feeling that every day together is precious. Who knows what might happen tomorrow?"

"What, down here in deepest Devon? We can't all be on the front line. I suppose I agree with you in a way, 'cos I feel so different having experienced war at first hand. I must be a first for a girl, having actually been in battle."

Her parents exchanged an odd glance at this and the silence lengthened. Finally, her father cleared his throat and said, "Not really. I don't suppose you have ever seen the scar up your mother's back, have you?"

"No, what caused that?"

"A shrapnel wound. Your mother was a sister in a front line casualty clearing station during the last war and was seriously injured when it was shelled."

"Mummy! I had no idea. Why didn't you ever tell us? No wonder my antics bother you a bit."

"More than a bit, dear. Your father and I made a deliberate decision to draw a veil over our doings in the last war because we wanted to put it all behind us. I very nearly died, y'know and to find you doing exactly the same this time round has really frightened us."

"Well I never. I'm so sorry, I had no idea."

"No dear, there was no reason why you should. We preferred to keep it quiet."

Her father cut in. "No doubt you think you are the only girl to have suffered such terrible hardships. I'm going to give you another book to read. It's called, *Not so Quiet – Stepdaughters of War* and it's a lightly fictionalised autobiography by a girl who was an ambulance driver in the last war. She worked in appalling brutalising conditions right on the front line with death, filth and destruction all around her. Your mother endured very similar conditions in the casualty clearing station. Once you've read that you won't feel quite so much of a pioneer. But a word of caution; we're not like the parents portrayed in the book. Proud of you, maybe; bombastic like them we are not. And if you don't believe it ask your Aunt Bidgie; she was an ambulance driver too in the last war."

"She was? But she's the most unwarlike creature imaginable. Her refinement must have suffered terribly."

Her mother cut in, "We all did dear, but in war you have to accept the rough side as well. I so hoped it would never happen again yet here we are, and I do not, I do not, I do not want my children to have to go through the same barbarity as we did." And she sat back with tears welling.

Jane sat up late utterly engrossed in the distressing tale from long ago and tried to imagine what it must have been like for her mother, and her aunt for that matter. It made Dunkirk seem almost civilised. But the descriptions of broken men, of screaming dying bodies, of gore and puss and vomit brought back her own nightmares and again she woke up in the middle of the night howling and groaning, with her mother holding her tight. There was a sudden overwhelming sense of kinship that she'd never had before with her strict, starchy mother and she clung to her, trembling and sobbing quietly.

"All right, all right, relax. You will get over these nightmares I promise you. I found that the worst tailed off quite quickly so you should get them behind you before long. Now take it easy."

"You had them too, mummy?"

"Yes, dear I did. It would be a very strange woman who didn't. One of the reasons I settled with your father was that he helped me deal with the remnants but before that I had bouts of them. Yours are faces; mine were stumps of arms and legs waving around."

"Oh mummy," and for a moment Jane regressed to little girl, burying her face in her mother's shoulder. Very gently her mother laid Jane down, stroked her hair and made soft crooning noises. And like a small child, Jane suddenly fell asleep again into a deep, dreamless sleep.

Heading into Plymouth next day Jane felt cleansed; somehow a dark shadow had lifted and she was able to enjoy the bright summer day. As they drove she chatted with her mother in a relaxed almost intimate way that she had never known before. A blockage had gone, the sense of shared experience and understanding transcending the parent to child barriers. Not to feel alone in her experience and to find kinship with her own mother, was giving Jane a stability, a re-connection to a safer and saner world that had been missing since she woke up in hospital. Suddenly, she could talk openly of death, of damaged bodies and deranged eyes, of finding herself indifferent to bombs and shells yet terrified by men's behaviour. And to do it woman to woman made it doubly powerful. Somehow the other woman being her own mother seemed less important than being able to unburden to someone who so clearly understood what she was talking about.

Plymouth was a quiet place. The traffic was sparse, people scurried about their business and the massed sandbags everywhere gave a strange defiant air to its streets. Shops were open but without the customers who had eddied around them in past times. Men with ARP (Air Raid Precautions) on their helmets stood around looking important for no obvious reason and naval uniforms were the only major sign of life about the place. Jane shuddered at the change.

When the twins came rampaging off the train, they took one look at a hatless Jane and shouted, "Jane's a badger, Jane's a badger," artlessly until she got cross and gave them both a clip across the ears. There was no mention of her scarred face. But it would take more than that to suppress their high spirits and the run home was full of noise from the back seat. But to Jane there was a comfort in the rowdy cheerfulness of childhood unconcerned with more than the world around them. Saturday brought another surprise; her sister Sarah suddenly walked in. Hugs of greeting done, she explained that the ballet course had finished early because of a bombing threat so she had simply taken the train home and caught a bus to their drive end. Jane smiled gently at her younger sister's enthusiasm, talking about the new steps she'd learnt, the tough approach of the Russian ballet mistress and how it had developed her abilities. All this Jane had some difficulty connecting with. Not so long ago a new ballet step would have been of enormous interest to her; now it seemed irrelevant. 'Will it keep you alive?' she wondered. But it was nice to see her kid sister again and Jane consciously thought, 'I must not spoil this enthusiasm with my sourness'.

And interesting, she thought, that not one of her siblings had commented about her scarred face. Sarah seemed to quite like the white streak. During the next couple of days Jane tried hard to re-connect with her beloved younger sister, but they were not on the same wavelength any more. "Jane, what is wrong with you? You never used to be as grumpy as this," her sister said to her. Jane could only shake her head, confused herself about what was wrong. The terrible weight she was carrying pushed out barriers, which only her mother seemed able to understand. To Sarah it was grumpiness; to the twins Jane had become another adult and hence the enemy.

CHAPTER 12:
Thinking

Jane was trying to make sense of her feelings when her father drove into the yard bearing Granny Beacon – his mother - and Aunt Bidgie. Granny Beacon was another long lean figure, a bit stooped from a lifetime of hard farm work, grey-haired and with a deeply lined care-worn face, but now all smiles at seeing her son and his family. She always complained that she didn't see nearly enough of her grandchildren, so there were special hugs and little presents for them all except Jane. This hurt Jane in a mild way but a week later all was explained when Granny produced a small bottle of perfume for her. "I'd bocht ye a wee toy thing but then I saw ye wer'na child ony mair so that wouldna dae. Good Goad Jane, ye've grown up in a hurry."

Jane could only smile sadly and give her granny a hug. 'A wee toy thing might have been rather fun' she thought wistfully. Aunt Bidgie was wafting about in her elegant way, talking to everyone, but from a distance. Her Buchan accent, long modified into an Edinburgh drawl, disguised a lively mind and enthusiasm for the things that enthused her; mainly classic clothing, musical theatre and the gin bottle. Looking at her with a new perspective Jane detected a deep sadness behind her sophisticated ways.

Three days after they arrived Jane found herself alone with her aunt in the snug after dinner. It was part of Aunt Bidgie's style never to ask questions or to show interest in other people, so Jane was about to ask her questions when she was startled to be asked straight out, "Jane, darling, have you considered doing something about that badger stripe?"

"Well yes, I had quite a debate about it when it first grew in, but the concensus was that it looked rather good."

"Couldn't you have decided for yourself?"

"Well, I suppose so, but I don't see myself like others do so I thought a few opinions might help. Don't you like it?"

Her aunt looked appraisingly from the depths of a comfy armchair, her iron-grey coif immaculately in place. She gently sank a large mouthful of gin, looked long at Jane and said, "Well, dear heart, I suppose it's different. But you'll never get away from being called Badger Beacon."

Jane rolled up her eyes. "Don't I know it. The twins have already given up any other names and I was getting more and more of it before I left Dover. But it is distinctive, isn't it?"

Having topped up her gin glass Aunt Bidgie looked at the stripe again. This bothered Jane, as she'd always thought of her aunt as a fount of good taste. "Distinctive certainly. Whether that's in your favour is another matter, but if that's what you want you'll have to get used to the consequences. You won't be able to hide in the crowd looking like that, y'know."

"Was I trying to hide in the crowd? That had never occurred to me, Aunt Bidgie. Maybe you're right but we'll have to see. It's interesting that it is the white streak people comment on, not the scars. I'd have thought the scars were the more powerful sight."

"Yes Jane, they are, but people don't like to comment on that and besides it's becoming quite common already to see people with wound scars. White streaks less so."

Jane saw an opening. "Aunt Bidgie, father gave me a book to read because he's trying to get me to see the war in a wider context. It's about female ambulance drivers on the front line in the last war and he said you were one of them. Were you really?"

Her aunt held up her gin glass. "See that? I don't like the stuff really but it eases the pain a lot. Yes, I was an ambulance driver and the book is pretty accurate, although I was fortunate in having a humane boss. When I went I was no more than a raw girl off the farm, but at least I was used to working outdoors and to driving things, which was more than most of the nice middle class girls from London who they threw into the job. Mostly, they lasted months at best. One or two toughs hung on and I did two years before I was invalided out."

"Invalided out? What happened to you? Was it like mother, a shelling?"

Aunty Bidgie shook her head slowly, sadly. "No, nothing so glamorous I'm afraid. My ambulance overturned one dark night and I was trapped under it in freezing water for nine hours. By the time they got me out I had raging pneumonia and by the time I'd recovered from that six months later the war was over. Far more people were lost to illness and accidents than ever were killed by the enemy, y'know. Your mother got several medals. All I had to show for the war to end all wars was permanently damaged lungs and a meaningless engagement ring. It was treating me that started your father specialising in chest medicine."

Jane butted in, "A meaningless engagement ring? Why was it meaningless?"

The gin glass was raised and half emptied in one long gulp. "Because he was killed two weeks before the end of the war. After that I joined that huge mass of women who outnumbered men and had no prospect of getting one. I've made a good life for myself because I had to, but there's still a bit of me would swap it for a partner. It's a lonely life, my dear."

It was Jane's turn to look long into the log fire, all this family revelation feeling a bit heavy.

"What do you think I should do, Aunt Bidgie? Before I came home I thought it was obvious but one way and another I'm having awfully serious doubts."

"Tell me, Jane darling, do you like what you're doing? The small scale reality of your own life should be the decider. You can't win the war on your own, but you can't avoid its consequences either. So, to my mind the best bet is to do something that you enjoy doing and hope that contributes to the great ant's nest."

Jane nodded slowly. "I love what I do on the boats and it looks like I'll be able to go on doing it. And being a pioneer is exciting and scary at the same time. I'm hoping the Admiralty will relent and let Wrens crew the harbour launches so the seamen can go off to fight. Not that they're necessarily keen. So, for that alone it's worth going on doing it. But the war and the death and destruction? Is that worth it? And should I contribute to it?"

"Jane, like I said, you can't avoid doing something and what you're doing sounds eminently good to me. But it might be wise if you didn't go looking for trouble as well. I remember you as a little girl; always impulsive and dashing off to do something without stopping to think about the consequences. Do you remember that time on the farm when you were still a wee bairn and decided that the bull was really rather a pet? You went into his field with a posy of wildflowers? It was all right until you tickled his nose with them then he got rather cross. All we could do was watch terrified from the gate as we were afraid going into the field would set the bull off. But at least you had the good sense to dodge from side to side as you ran away. You have been prone to pushing your luck all along and it seems you haven't changed."

Jane laughed, "Ye gods, do I remember it? I was terrified and I can still feel his breath down my neck. I think he let me off in the end, knowing I was just a kid."

"You brought it on yourself, darling, like your present horrors. Once you've experienced violence you can never be quite the same again and that will always lie on your consciousness. With a wheen of determination you can get beyond it, but now you have to live with it. If you accept that and that it will always be a part of you then you'll be well on your way to a good life again because there are happier parts as well. Your present sadness isn't all of you, Jane, simply a lump in your heart."

Jane sighed. "That's a comfort, I suppose and at least the nightmares are getting less vivid. Thank you, aunt, I think you've helped me see things more clearly and I like that there can be some happiness again. Recently it hasn't seemed like that. Why do you think father is doing this to me?"

Aunt Bidgie shrugged, took another generous gulp of gin and said, "Your father's hatred of violence runs very deep. I haven't asked him, but if I know him half as well as I think I do, he's trying to get you to see that war is not a nice business. I suspect he doesn't want to see you becoming some sort of Amazon warrior, which you seemed to be drifting towards."

Jane shook her head in puzzlement. "But I was only doing my bit, Aunt Bidgie."

"No you weren't. I have not heard much about your exploits at Dunkirk but what I have heard seems well outside 'doing your bit' if I understand the stories correctly. Did you enjoy being there?"

"Enjoyment didn't come into it. There was a job to do and I got on with it. There were times when I felt good about the men I'd rescued and the donkey, but I'm not sure that was enjoyment."

"Jane darling, you have been through a lot for someone so young and getting it all into balance won't be easy. But your father is trying to get you to see this whole business in context, I suspect. My generation have deep mental scars from what we went through. We all hoped so much your life would not have to suffer in the same way, yet here you are, covered in scars already and struggling with a pain in your heart we never thought would come again. Some of your father's behaviour is to cover a deep disappointment – not with you – but with a world that is putting his children through the same brutal mill he went through. To him it is important that you understand the wider scene in which you're acting your part. At least that should give you some handles on which to hang your experiences as this ghastly war goes on. With any luck, that will allow you to survive and stay sane in it. Now it's a painful process but if you emerge strengthened, then he will have done you an enormous favour. I only pray that he's got it right."

"Well thanks, Aunt Bidgie. Right now it doesn't feel like it but I kind of see what you're getting at, I think. Oh well, back to the *Iliad.*"

Aunt Bidgie smiled, picked up her glass and departed, leaving Jane to stare into the fire, now burnt down to glowing embers. 'All right father,' she thought 'you will not defeat me.'

The next morning the postman called as usual and Jane went into the kitchen to see if there was any mail for her. She was startled to hear Agnes give a great shriek and sit down heavily at the table trembling violently. She had been drinking a cup of tea but was now struggling to hold it. "Oh, Agnes, what now?"

"Miss Jane, Miss Jane, I've had a letter from Gianni. He's alive! He says the authorities got it all wrong about who survived the torpedoing and he was one of the lucky ones who got brought back. But now he tells me he's being sent off in another ship to Canada, but at least he's alive."

"Agnes, that's wonderful! Or at least it's partly wonderful. I suppose we have to keep our fingers crossed for the next trip but at least you're not a widow yet. We must keep hoping."

Agnes nodded mutely and managed to get the cup to her lips. "Can I help you, Agnes?" Asked Jane trying to get hold of the cup. But Agnes held on to it resolutely and shook her head. "Thanks, Miss Jane, I'll be all right in a minute. It's all a bit much to take in."

At this moment her mother came in.

"Mummy, have you heard about Pappa Gianni? Apparently he's alive after all. Isn't that wonderful?"

"Good Lord, how did that happen?"

Agnes had to explain it all again. Her mother gave the trembling heap a hug, patted her on the shoulder and said, "Well, that is good news. Perhaps you can get back on your feet now, Agnes."

This got a wan smile, but already there was a firmness about her, which had been missing. "I'll miss him but it's better than having him dead."

With this drama settling down Jane went into the breakfast room to find Aunt Bidgie on her own. Again, Agnes' story had to be re-told.

Aware of how unfit she was, Jane had been going walking each day and was pleased when her aunt offered to join her after breakfast. As they went, the sophisticated city lady reverted to farm girl and showed Jane things she'd never known about the wild flowers, the trees, the wildlife and the weather. They talked about anything, in fact, except the war. Physically, Jane was getting better rapidly and her return to duty could not be far away. The nightmares had eased and her father had left Jane to pull books off the shelf as she chose. As peace was descending inside her, her brother David arrived home, tanned and fit. He'd been sailing on the River Dart, going out to sea no longer being allowed and was as full as ever of enthusiasm for being on the water. He took one look at Jane's scarred face, shook his head sadly then never mentioned it again. It was his idea to row up to *Osprey* and see how she was faring. They found her remarkably unchanged; the laying-up procedures had been well done and she was standing up nicely. Jane got a real tug of nostalgia seeing the boat quietly lying in the creek and thought longingly of the day she could be opened up and set sailing again. Right at that moment it looked a long way away. They pumped her out, not that there was much water in her bilge, cleaned the seagull droppings off the canvas cover and checked that the mooring ropes were still in good order, then left the old boat to its quiet rustication. Feeling it was high time she exercised more of herself. Jane did the rowing and twinges from ribs and shoulder hole suggested that she wasn't quite completely healed. But the hole in her shoulder had now grown out as much as it was going to, the skin was forming over it and soon it too would be mended. Jane found the visit to *Osprey* thoroughly unsettling, and struggled to be enthusiastic at the dinner table.

The next day her father came in looking even grimmer than usual. "Jane, David" he said, "we have a job to do. I've hired *Shalima* to the Navy for the duration, but we have to take her over to Guzz this weekend. You will be crewing." His forty-foot motor cruiser had been lying quietly in their boathouse since the start of the war, Doctor Beacon hanging on hoping that the war wouldn't last. But by July 1940, it was plain they were in for a long haul unless Germany succeeded in invading Britain, in which case it might be ended a lot quicker. In the quiet peace of rural Devon, the war seemed a long way away but the news filtering through was not good. Invasion scares came and went each day, church bells were only to be rung if an invasion did happen, every signpost in England disappeared and the first basic attempts at invasion barriers were started. They would not have deterred the *Wehrmacht* for long if they had managed to get ashore on the South Coast but were a gesture. As ever, Britain's best defence was the twenty-one mile ditch called the Dover Strait and again Jane thought of Jamie's quote about Napoleonic invasions scares; "I do not say they cannot come, sir. I only say they cannot come by sea." That old Admiral had it about right, hoped Jane.

Jane found herself being included with the adults after dinner, which was nice in a way, but a bit dull. The conversation tended to be slow and heavy and full of doom and Jane found herself rebelling.

"Do you mind if I go and chat with David?" she asked.

"We don't mind in the least dear, but isn't it time you accepted that you're grown up?"

A little dam burst in Jane's mind. "Mummy, I'm only twenty. I want to laugh and dance and be carefree and what I've got inside me is bad enough without having to behave as though I'm an old fuddy-duddy because of it. I've got to have more in my life, please." And she looked pleadingly at the assembled group.

"All right dear. Off you go." Contrarily, Jane felt resentment at her mother airily dismissing her like a small child and seemingly unmoved by her outburst. From there David and she cooked up a ploy to escape and for several nights they missed dinner, always remembering to tell their mother they would be out. David took his fiddle, Jane her accordion and they got their local pub, The Dolphin's regulars singing noisily.

Greatly cheered up, Jane was singing as noisily when they went aboard *Shalima.* Her father eyed her, "I'd say you are about ready to be passed fit, I'm afraid. Let's see how you do on the trip to Guzz." For Jane the trip was simply a pleasure, a moving deck and sea air stirring a powerful yen to be back in her job and busy in her own element. This was the first time she'd been properly afloat since she tied up P36 back in Dover Harbour, she realised with a start. What a distant memory that seemed. Arriving at flagstaff steps, Jane ran up the steps, into the Boats Officer's office, came to attention and saluted, forgetting that she was in plain clothes and didn't have a hat on. The Boats Officer, who had quietly had a lot to do with Jane's early success in *Amaryllis*, looked mildly surprised. "Ah, Beacon, how nice to see you again. I gather you've been having an adventurous time since last I saw you."

"Well yes sir, you could say that." She was about to go on about her exploits when her father came into office. Then it was "Johnny, good to see you again. Your young lady here has been trying to remember her drill."

"Hello, Tom, funny times we're living in, aren't they? I've brought *Shalima* for you. Do look after her, won't you?"

"Johnny, for you I'll treat her like my own. I've arranged the best Chief in Guzz for Cox'n. Take her round to the dock and stick her in the top corner, will you? I'm afraid she will have to be painted grey all over." Her elegant white hull and sparkling varnished topsides were about to disappear.

Johnny Beacon winced but nodded. "All right, I'll have her smartened up again one of these days." And twenty minutes later they had handed her over to a Petty Officer and were squeezed into the Austin Ruby, her father walking out of the dockyard without a backward glance. Back at the Grange, he looked hard at Jane. "Young lady, I rather think it is time for me to sign you off. Much as we'd love to keep you here, I am afraid I have run out of medical excuses and it's time for you to go back to your duty. I'll be writing to Superintendent Welby to that effect tomorrow."

Which is how, farewells said, Jane found herself back in uniform and across a desk from Mrs Welby. Not for the first time this lady had Jane's service record spread out on her desk. "Well, Beacon, more adventures and more medals, I see. But don't let that fool you into thinking the Admiralty loves you now. It doesn't. I have heard of at least one Admiral agitating to have you slung out, so if I were you I would keep a low profile and quietly go about your business."

These references meant little to Jane. For all her recent reading, she was seriously out of touch with naval current affairs and could only wait patiently for Mrs Welby to continue. "Headquarters have decreed that you should go back to Dover to continue boat work there and Chief Officer Currie has agreed to have you. I gather she feels that you may find some sort of redemption there."

Jane was even more puzzled. Medals? Admirals? Redemption? What was all this about? She had been hoping simply to be told to go back to serving on a boat somewhere and continue with the great experiment. It seemed this was going to happen but what was the rest of it about? But she knew well enough by now not to ask that kind of question so she simply nodded. Mrs Welby looked her very directly in the eye. "You do seem subdued by your own standards. No arguments? No difficult questions?"

Jane could only shake her head, but something seemed to be expected so she said, "No ma'am. Recent experience has left me a bit out of touch I think, so the sooner I'm back on a boat and actively back in the Wrens the better. I think I'm fully healed now and ready to go." This seemed to satisfy her interrogator who nodded and said, "Mrs Jones has your travel warrant and draft chit. Good luck." And with a nod of dismissal she turned back to her intray.

Later, sitting on her kitbag and Rufus, her large teddy bear, in a train's corridor, Jane tried to make sense of her jumbling thoughts.

> *To fight, or not to fight,*
> *That is the question.*
> *Is it right that my bit should cause*
> *Pain, even death, to other people?*
> *Or do I want to give my life,*
> *still to be lived*
> *To a war I am told has to be fought?*
> *Death comes so easily*
> *Surviving not so.*
> *I suppose I see why*
> *The forces of evil must be defeated.*
> *And yet, and yet... my life is new,*
> *My wish to live overwhelming.*
> *Is that so bad? Can I not live,*
> *And love and be a vibrant creature?*
> *Why must I offer this soft young body of mine*
> *To bullet and bomb,*
> *So that our elders can quaff their brandy*
> *In peace? Peace! Ha! Is that not a mirage*
> *A perversion of our urge to live?*
> *Will I go on? I suppose I must,*
> *There Is No Alternative.*
> *Or so they say.*

PART FOUR:

UNDER THE BATTLE

CHAPTER 13:
Going Up

Coming back into the cool of the Dover Wrennery was a pleasure after a long hot crowded train journey. Jane reported to the Quarters Officer on arrival.

"Ah Beacon, welcome back. I gather you will be returning to the boats and living here again. Please, don't steal the food this time."

"Ma'am, the food was the least of what I took last time."

"I know Beacon, but it was the food that upset me most."

"All right ma'am, I've taken a vow to be a good girl so hopefully I won't be a problem to you."

"I am relieved to hear it. You will be back in the same killick's cabin you were in before. There have been some changes of personnel but you'll find mostly things are the same as they were. Now, Chief Officer Currie wants to see you tomorrow morning to discuss what you will be doing. Be at her office at 0915."

Jane smiled sweetly and went off to her cabin. Barbara's bunk with its crucifix and holy picture was the same and Jo was evidently still there judging by the picture of an elderly destroyer over her bunk. Of Esther there was no sign. The other two bunks appeared empty so Jane opted for the one she'd had before and unpacked, hanging her tattered ensign over the bunk end and sitting Rufus at the head. Jane looked at the large stuffed bear with some irony. She'd never been given to soft toys as a child apart from a well-loved sea horse, but because of his history Rufus was a bit special. The place was very quiet and Jane wondered where the off duty watch were. She had been accustomed to there always being some noise and chatter about.

When Jo came in later it became clear; the watch keepers had largely been moved elsewhere, most of the Wrens in this building were now day working secretarial and support staff and were at work. Jo and Barbara were expecting to move to join their watches very shortly, but it was nice to see Jane again before they moved on.

"And Esther? Where has she gone?"

"Oh, gone for officer training. It eventually dawned on the hierarchy that a brain like hers could be more usefully employed than leading a teleprinter watch."

"Oh well, good luck to her. I'm going back in the boats, I believe. How are you doing?"

Jo smiled. "Still going with my jaunty, although I don't see that much of him now. The Navy's very largely cleared out of Dover and he's based at Portsmouth. But we manage to see each other every now and then. Since Dunkirk the pressure's eased off hugely in the tunnels and we get along nicely with half the girls in each watch. It's really quite easy now, but I've put in for a transfer to Portsmouth."

"But I thought you were an immobile?"

"I was but I've taken a chance and gone mobile. Knowing the Wrens they'll probably send me to the North of Scotland but it's worth a try."

Jane gave her an ironic lift of an eyebrow in response.

In her best doeskin uniform, Jane was finishing her burgoo next morning when all manner of violent explosions suddenly erupted. A wave of German bombers was attacking the shipping in the harbour, or what few remnants of it they could find. For ten minute it was pandemonium, ships on fire and sinking with very limited gunfire in response as the German planes roamed more or less at will over the harbour. Then, quiet fell except for the roar of flames and odd bits of ordnance cooking off. The wail of the *Stukas* had brought back bad memories for Jane and for a few minutes she got very tense, but as the planes went she decided to carry on as ordered and made sure she was outside her OiC's office by five past nine. At thirteen minutes past a Wren writer emerged, asked, "Leading Wren Beacon?" and on getting a nod said, "Come this way, please."

Entering her Queen Bee's office at 0915 exactly and noting she had her hat on, Jane came smartly to attention, saluted and reported, "1095 Leading Wren Beacon ma'am". Chief Officer Currie returned the salute, took off her hat and said, "Yes, Beacon, I think I know you by now. Take a seat please."

Jane did as bidden and waited.

"Right, Beacon, we have agreed that you will go back to serving on the boats here. My main concern is to try to return your activities to some semblance of normality. There are to be no more heroics, is that understood?" And she looked Jane very directly in the eye. Jane could only shrug.

"Your position has been discussed at some length with Wren headquarters and naval staff here. We have decided to continue with your boat crew work here in Dover Harbour for some months yet, although there is a possibility of your going to Nore Command in the New Year. Superintendent Carpenter is following the experiment with close interest and has suggested that she would like to bring you to the Thames at some stage. I've also had a discussion with our boats officer about what to do with you. It is clear that you are capable of any job in a boat except Stoker and we don't see a lot of point in your simply carrying on as a boat hand."

Alarm bells rang in Jane's mind. If not as a boat hand, then what? She knew of boat crew being diverted into the bosun's stores and spending their lives splicing ropes, which was not an appealing prospect. She wilted slightly with concern. But Chief Officer Currie continued.

"So, we have decided that you can be Cox'n of your own boat, and the little skimmer is being assigned to you."

"Oh wow," suddenly the sun had come out and Jane perked up. "You mean I'm to get *Titch* for myself? That would be something."

"Yes, Beacon we do mean that. You will have an AB assigned to you as crew."

"Oh, couldn't I have another Wren? Then we really would be making progress."

Chief Officer Currie smiled, a gentle sympathetic smile of encouragement. "Beacon, if you can come up with a suitable Wren we'll consider it. But tomorrow you will have an AB from the boat pool."

"Right ma'am, I'll have to see about that one. Might I be able to get a list of Wrens based here? Maybe I could pick out someone."

"You can look at the list here, but it is not to leave my office. Good luck and Beacon, please try to keep out of trouble."

Jane shook her head in frustration. Why was she always being warned to keep out of trouble? It was not as though she went looking for it.

"Boats Officer is expecting to see you this morning so I suggest you go there directly after this."

She established that it would be several days before she could look at the Wrens list, so headed back to the harbour and into the boats office, which was unscathed despite the violence which had gone on close by it earlier. To her surprise Stan was sitting behind a desk shuffling bits of paper. He jumped up when Jane came in. "Hello lass, nice to see you again. I heard you were coming back." On impulse she gave him a big hug noting how he went pink.

"What are you doing behind a desk, Stan? Not your place really, is it?"

"I'm filling in for chiefie here while he's on leave. And you'd be surprised, I can really be quite comfy behind a desk."

Jane gave him an ironic smile. "I'm told Boats Officer wants to see me. Can I do that now?"

"Wait one lass and I'll check."

Stan emerged from the inner sanctum five minutes later. "He says he'll be about half an hour. Care for a cup of coffee while you wait?"

She fell to gossiping with Stan and caught up on all the local doings. Summoned to the Boats Officer's presence, Jane remembered her drill and waited. "Good morning Beacon. You have already seen your Chief Officer?"

Jane nodded. "Yes sir, earlier this morning."

"Good. So, you will know that we have decided to see how you do with your own boat. From tomorrow you will be Cox'n of the skimmer. With so few Navy ships here courtesy of the Luftwaffe, Our boat establishment has been cut back.

The picket boat and *Amaryllis* are both used to operate more widely, liaising with convoys and the like and one whaler plus the skimmer are sufficient inside. But they are kept busy and you will find there's plenty to do. I've taken care to choose a reliable AB to work with you."

Jane cut in here. "That's good sir. Chief Officer Currie said that if I could find a suitable Wren you'd consider crewing the skimmer with her instead. Is that right?"

"We discussed it and I have no problems in principle if she's as good as you. But it would need to be a very suitable Wren who knows boats already and what's more has a good grasp of engines; I gather you don't know much about them."

"I'm afraid not, sir. I've learned a little, but nothing like enough to look after one."

"That's what I thought. Be here at 0630 tomorrow ready to start and we'll see how it goes from there."

Jane saluted. "Aye aye, sir."

Outside, she took a look at the boat berths. The skimmer and the picket boat were alongside, and she could see the whaler out in the harbour where indeed there were very few ships. Tucked up in the corner were the pulling cutter and whalers, evidently still not used. Dover was virtually empty of warships because the *Luftwaffe* had bombed and harried them so much they had been withdrawn to the Nore and to Portsmouth, a few days before Jane returned. They were no longer so crucially needed at Dover so it made sense to move them. Destroyers still popped in and out on anti-invasion patrol and the coastal forces boats based there were growing in number, but the mass presence had gone. Despite this, Dover remained a viable harbour throughout the war and was never closed.

With the rest of the day clear Jane took a walk into the town and found a highly charged atmosphere. Down in rural Devon the threat of invasion had seemed remote, as had the general war fever. The radio might bring daily doses of invasion scares, but they did little to disturb the even tenor of life at the Old Grange. But in Dover, Jane was plunged into something else entirely. There was a tense nervousness in the air, a febrile feeling of living on the edge of disaster. This tension was heightened by a second bombing raid in the early afternoon, but again the harbour was the focus and the town unaffected.

Only twenty-one miles away, clearly visible from Dover, a major invasion fleet was assembling. That it was a ramshackle affair of canal barges and unsuitable boats did nothing to lessen the tension throughout Britain. The *Wehrmacht's* conviction after the Dunkirk debacle that it was invincible and that to win all it had to do was launch itself across the water, was echoed in Britain. Spy hysterias raged, the newspapers stoked up the general sense of impending doom and as Pappa Gianni had found, foreigners of any sort were given a very hard time of it.

* * *

In truth, the German war machine could only have succeeded if it had crossed the Channel within a few weeks of Dunkirk while Britain was still reeling chaotically from the disaster which had befallen its forces. Once Britain had time to draw breath it was ready to withstand any German incursion, even if the breath was drawn a bit tremulously. But that was not commonly known and the threat of Operation Sealion – the German plan to invade Britain – hung over the country until well into the Autumn. For a few crucial months, only Churchill's rhetoric kept up spirits. Yet there was a curious defiance in the air as well. Almost, a sense of exhilaration that Britain was the only country now defying the mighty German war machine and an enormous pride in standing alone against it. Talking to people in the street she found an atmosphere of 'we can take it, we can beat 'em if they try to come'. Mixed with the fear and worry was a dogged determination and a sense that every day was precious. Whereas each day would normally have passed by as 'just another day', now there was sense of living in the midst of great times and every day was another scene in some grand drama.

* * *

Back in the Wrennery and heading towards the mess room for supper, Jane heard what sounded like a familiar voice. "Oi tell you, we can do any of that." Startled and intrigued, Jane rounded the corner to see the back of a very large Wren ahead of her. That could only be one person and she went up to it and gave the back a hearty slap. "Hello Punch." But that was almost a mistake. Punch whirled round, dropping into a defensive crouch with fists raised at the ready. She pulled up short of letting fly, but only just. "Jane! Ye gods, don't do that. You nearly got a broken nose to add to your scars. Please don't come up on me like that."

Startled, Jane stepped back. "Sorry Punch, I had no idea it would bother you. But it's great to see you, what are doing here?"

"I'm first draft visual signaller now. That's better than just being a messenger." Punch looked closely at Jane. "Your letters said you'd got knocked about a bit but your face really is a mess. Are you all right now?"

"Oh yes, passed fit for service and back in the boats tomorrow." Not surprisingly, Jane's mind had been racing ahead. "Punch, I'm getting my own boat from tomorrow. Just the skimmer, but that's fine for a start. They've said I can have a Wren for crew if I can find somebody suitable. Would you like to do it?"

"Would Oi ever. Do you really think there's a chance?"

"One other thing. Do you know anything about engines?"

Punch considered this. "A bit, I s'ppose. Used to help me Dad work on them an' he explained what he was doing, so yes you could say so."

"So, you could look after the skimmer's little petrol engine? A car engine really."

"Oh yes, no problem."

"Good. In that case I'll ask if I can have you for crew."

And that was how Punch became Boating Wren number two. To Boats Officer's query if she could do the job, Jane simply introduced Wren Violet Johnson who towered above the other people in the boats office. Boats Officer, having already heard about her background, took one look at her and forgot any further enquiry about whether she was up to the job. A week later, fully kitted out with bell bottoms, white lanyard and size ten sea boots, Punch joined *Titch* for the first time and as Jane had expected, performed well from the start. "Y'know, Punch I'm not terribly religious, but your turning up like you did really was some sort of providence. It couldn't have happened better and I almost wonder if there's some hand in the background quietly arranged this."

"Don't think so Jane. When I finished me signals course I was drafted to Dover. No-one said anything about boats."

"No probably not, but it really is a remarkable co-incidence."

Boat hook drill, when to hook on, and the correct ceremonial for senior officers were about all that Jane had to teach Punch and within a week they were working happily as a team. Punch's life on a Thames barge showed through very rapidly in the way she automatically caught and threw ropes, tied knots, balanced on the boat and was completely comfortable on the water. Although Jane didn't know it, the AB – a seasoned two badge boatman – who had been with her until Punch arrived, reported highly on her performance both in handling the boat and in how she gave her orders to him. Simple, direct and clear was how he described them. She had shown no fear in giving orders to a man and in truth that aspect had not even occurred to her; she got on with it naturally and without fuss. It never entered her head that she was on trial with him. With the change of crew hand came a change of atmosphere, of greater enthusiasm to go with the professionalism. Coming alongside at the end of a long day, Punch turned to Jane, beamed and said, "This is what I joined up for." Jane's first reaction was to think, 'Just wait till it's cold wet and windy and you won't be so keen' then thought again 'Punch, with a lifetime afloat? I'll bet it makes no difference.' And that proved true too.

But in Dover in early August it was hot and the girls found a blue shirt, black tie and uniform jacket a bit much. Punch, eyeing the few matelots going about their business, remarked, "Y'know Jane, we could wear our white cottons too. If the sailors can I'm sure we can."

"What a good idea. I'd wondered what we should do with them but yes, you're right; if they can we can."

The square-necked white shirt with its distinctive blue edging known as a cotton or white front was universal warmer weather rig for the lower deck, worn with white shorts in the tropics and over bell bottoms in home waters in summer. Next morning the pioneer boat Wrens also emerged in their cottons, their white lanyards round their waists in imitation of what the men did. During the day no-one said anything, treating the sight as normal, but when they came into their quarters in the evening they were pounced on by the Quarters Officer.

"And what do you two think you are wearing?"

"Our white cottons, ma'am. They are part of our uniform issue for warmer weather."

"Indeed. But they are not Wren uniform and I'm not at all sure I can permit this."

"It's only the same rig as the sailors wear, ma'am and in our experimental status we follow what they do because it's the most practical."

"That may be so and I can see why you do it. But it will need to be sanctioned so I'm going to pass a query up the line. "

Their Quarters Officer was actually quite a sensible and practical lady; outside of the Wrens she was a kind and caring housewife and mother of teenage children and she struggled sometimes to stick to the Wren regulations too rigidly. She scowled at the pair and said, "All right, in view of the heat I shan't force you back into Wren uniform yet, but you will have to abide by any ruling that comes from authority."

"Yes ma'am, we understand that."

That night Jane drafted a short letter to headquarters explaining how practical the cotton was in warm weather and how it was no more than what the sailors wore anyway. She got Punch to write out a fair copy in her elegant copperplate and popped it into the letterbox next morning as they headed down to the harbour. Hopefully, it would be in the correct pair of hands before the formal request worked its way up the system from her Quarters Officer.

After a busy day round the harbour Jane was peacefully eating her supper, her mind still out on the water, when Punch plonked down next to her and asked, "Jane, would you like to meet me oppo?" Startled at the idea that Punch would have an oppo, Jane said, "Yes of course," and was even more startled to be introduced to a tiny scrawny-looking Wren. "Jane, This is Sparrer."

"Pleased ter meechya."

Jane looked mildly puzzled. "Sparrer? Is that your name?"

"Naw, but that's what I'm known as. Y'know, like the bird."

The light came on in Jane's mind. "Oh, you mean sparrow?" The girl was a bit bird-like with sharp features and darkly bright inquisitive eyes beneath a mop of black hair.

"That's right, Sparrer."

"Are you a real Cockney?"

"More or less, from Bermondsey. Me dad works in the docks there."

"What are you doing in the Wrens?"

"I'm a messenger. Me an' Punch were together at Pompey and managed to get drafted together."

Punch cut in. "We go well together. She's the brains, Oi'm the brawn. We've had some real fun in the pubs at night."

'I'll bet you have' thought Jane, but kept the thought to herself.

"Sparrow's fine, but what's your official name?"

Sparrer laughed. "Euphemia Jack, but I can't remember when anyone 'cept me mum called me that. I'm Phemie to her."

"It is a bit of a mouthful, isn't it?"

By now they'd finished their 'whales on a raft' (sardines on toast) so they split up, Punch and oppo to head for the bright lights, Jane to retire to her cabin where she met Barbara for the first time in days.

"Hello Barbara, how are things?"

"Oh, nice, Jane. Job's a lot easier now the pressure is off and what do you think, I'm, getting engaged."

"You are? That's wonderful. Who to?"

"The Jimmy in the *Medway Queen.*" Do you remember him? We've both found God and are ever so happy doing it together."

"Doing what together?"

"Worshipping God of course. But we've really been quite naughty. We got weekend leave a couple of weeks ago and slipped into the back of the church and do you know what? We held hands."

"Barbara, you didn't!"

"Oh yes, we did, so we thought that if God allowed us to hold hands in his holy place, perhaps he was telling us to get married too. Do you think you can get pregnant from holding hands?"

"You what? Barbara, really." Jane took a deep breath. "No you can't, you can be sure of that."

But Jane was thinking, 'if she's that ignorant, how on earth are they going to manage being married?'

But all she said was, "Good luck with it, Barbara. Sounds like you'll need it. Do you know anything about married love?"

"Oh, God will guide us."

'That,' thought Jane, 'is highly unlikely, but who am I to spoil her innocence?' The notion of God as a sex tutor rather tickled Jane but that depth of ignorance troubled her as she settled for the night, thinking about what had been said to the gentle murmour of Barbara saying her prayers.

CHAPTER 14:
Old and New

With the lessening pressure on the boats it was not usually necessary to work *Titch* on a two crew basis and the boat was given over entirely to Jane and Punch. This meant an 0630 start and getting finished for the day around 1800 all going well, which made for long days and infrequent visits to the dining table, but the two girls were deeply happy in their little boat. It also meant that mostly the evenings were free so Jane turned her mind to a social life again. Out of curiosity she tried a night in the pub with Punch and Sparrer. The sight of Punch flirting outrageously with sailors half her size was something unexpected, but Punch remarked that after years of sailing in and out of the London docks she was used to socialising with seamen. Jane found the evening a bit crude for her taste, but noticed that the matelots gathering round Punch and Sparrer treated her with a good deal more reserve. In part, they knew of her and showed an instinctive respect. But in part, and despite the air of chumminess, she could not help feeling that they didn't really see her as one of them. Jane also tried the Saturday night 'Grab and Grope' and found it well named. It was lovely to be dancing again, but some of the attentions were fairly primitive and direct. Given her level of experience she wasn't too troubled by the raw sexuality of it, but found little to enjoy in wandering hands and beery bodies pressing up close.

Meantime, she discovered a little roof valley at the top of the Wrennery that was easy to get to, so in the hot summer weather she spent some of her time off sunbathing in this quiet corner recovering the tan she had largely lost since the previous year. A weather beaten and brown freckly face was one thing, a decent tan on her body much more precious. But what was a girl to do for a social life? The notice board, which had once been plastered with wardroom invitations, was now empty. Jo had lost her entree into the Chiefs' social circle when her jaunty's ship had moved to Portsmouth and she seemed content to write long letters then visit her family for the evening. Even the cinema on your own was less fun somehow, which meant it was start again time. Salvation peeped out in the form of an invitation to a party by the Dover Naval medical fraternity. 'Don't they have enough nurses?' wondered Jane but on enquiring was told they liked a bit of variety sometimes. She had fond memories of how they had looked after her so, without giving it much further thought, she signed up for it. What she hadn't bargained on was Jamie waiting at the door for her. "Hello Jane, how lovely to see you again. I heard you were back in town."

Jane smiled a little uncertainly. "Hello Jamie. Yes, I'm back in the boats here. Are you still at the hospital?"

"Yes, but I've been promoted ever so slightly. It is quiet round here now that all the ships have gone and I've put in for a fresh posting but who knows when that will happen. Would you like a drink?"

"Yes please, a pink gin."

Jane had been going to mingle, but Jamie stuck to her.

"Jane, I think I made the biggest mistake of my life, rejecting you. I have missed you so much. Tell me, have you missed me or have you been with some other men in the meantime?"

"No Jamie, I have not and if your dirty little mind is only going to dig like that you can clear off now."

He recoiled at the vehemence coming at him. "I'm sorry, Jane, I'm sorry. It's just that I have been longing for you and hoping that we might get together again."

"No chance Jamie. You rejected me once and that's enough. A girl's got some pride, y'know."

He looked deeply disappointed. "But if you've been with other men does that matter?"

"Listen, you obsessive creep, I have not been with anyone else meantime, I do not spread it around anyway and the one lover I have had was a man I was deeply attached to. You've obviously got me fixed in your mind as some sort of good time girl, but it simply isn't true."

"But you were willing to go to bed with me; you suggested it!"

"Did you notice the word 'love' slipping into our talk? That was why and for no other reason. Now calm down and accept that you've had your chance and blown it."

"Oh Jane, how sad."

"Yes isn't it, but not half as sad as the idea you obviously have of me. I'll be more careful in future." Across the room she spotted Sister Donaldson, gave her a wave, excused herself quickly from a crestfallen Jamie and greeted her healer. In her smart number one uniform Sister Donaldson was an impressive sight. The lady ran a practised eye over Jane's face and nodded with some satisfaction. "It's healing up very nicely, isn't it?"

"I'm not sure that anyone else would say nicely, but I suppose it's neat and tidy and fading all the time. I can't really ask for more, can I?"

Sister Donaldson laughed. "Well, I feel good about it anyway. I presume you're back in harness now?"

Jane nodded and gave the lady the story. After chatting for some time the Sister suddenly said, "The only other casualty was Doctor MacWhirter. He went into a steep decline after you left and he's never really been the same since."

"Well, that was his own silly fault. If he'd been a bit more accepting we might be together now. But I'm not giving him a second chance. Y'know, the stuff you taught me was great and I'm sure it will stand me in good stead, but there are times when I still don't get what it is that drives men. I thought it was only an urge to get off with you, but it seems to be more complex, or maybe less?"

"I gave up trying to do more than predict their behaviour patterns a long time ago."

"But they're not predictable, apart from the obvious, are they?"

"Oh, I'm not so sure about that. They might want virginal purity in their girl friend, but at the same time they want an enthusiastic bedmate and don't seem able to see that the two may not go together. That is predictable."

"I'll remember it. I'm certainly keeping out of mischief for now and the more I see of how men are, the more I think I ought to be very careful."

"That's what I told you."

The two laughed into each other's eyes. It was the first time Jane had seen the strict ward sister relax and laugh out loud and it took ten years off her appearance.

Back in the Wrennery with thirty seconds to spare for signing in, Jane got herself a late evening kye and sat by her bunk contemplating. It had been nice to get out and socialise and she felt again how cramped her life was, but the conversation with Jamie had been deeply disturbing. How could he think her a good time girl? And if he did, did other people see her the same way? It was one thing not to be a virginal innocent, quite another to be seen as a loose woman. Drifting off to sleep, she resolved to be very careful.

Those first few weeks back at Dover were a strange time for Jane. *Titch* was kept busy enough, running personnel ashore, taking urgent stores and messages and serving the gun batteries based on the detached breakwater. But the enormous pressure she had been used to, was gone. Instead of ships there were wrecks, some with masts and funnels sticking out of the water, others under the surface and marked by green buoys, which Jane had to memorise. Especially after dark, it was essential to know where they all were. Dotted round the harbour were no few small cargo ships lying alongside, badly bomb damaged in passing convoys and waiting to be removed for repair. Even the old *Sandhurst,* the depot ship, had its bombed and scorched carcass removed to the Thames for a much-needed rebuild. Outside the harbour coastal convoys plodded past and in the weeks before Jane returned there had been fierce action over them as the *Stukas* sank ship after ship with very little interference from the Royal Air Force.

* * *

This lack of interference was not accidental. The Luftwaffe was only marginally interested in the convoys of little coasters, which plodded past their noses, except as target practise. What they were trying to do was tempt the RAF fighters into the air so the huge swarms of German fighters could engage them in aerial combat, in the hope of reducing the British numbers so much they would not be able to mount much defence when the Luftwaffe moved inland. But in charge of Britain's Fighter Command was a man very well aware that was what the Germans were up to. Air Chief Marshal Sir Hugh ("Stuffy") Dowding refused to be drawn and kept his fighter force intact for the greater battle to come. But that was scant comfort to the ships under the lash from the air with only their own guns for defence.

* * *

By the end of July, interest in Dover itself was tailing off as the *Luftwaffe* moved its bombing campaign elsewhere, but it had lasting effects on the seamen underneath. Dover harbour had been bombed regularly and not long after Jane returned there had been one sudden flash raid on the port, a lone single-engined plane roaring over from landward dropping one bomb which blew chunks off the detached mole but did no serious harm. It was over so quickly no-one had time to react and Jane in mid-harbour had been too fascinated to feel fear until after it had gone. Then on 11th August a flight of twin-engined aircraft flew in low and straight as the girls were getting up. Again, the harbour was bombed quickly and the planes gone before anyone could react but there was very little in the way of targets left for them.

Titch's speed meant it often got last minute rush jobs to do and dashing round the harbour in a hurry became normal. It was around then that Stan gave Jane a large envelope of orders for a newly arrived destroyer as first job in the morning.

"These are for *HMS Skate*. You must hand them to her Commanding Officer, personally."

"*Skate*? Has it got wheels or something?"

"No lass, but it is a bit different. She's the oldest destroyer in active service. I did a commission in her in the mid '20s and at the time she seemed quite reasonable. Now, she's a museum piece, but has a fiercely loyal crew. Funny how defending something like that can get to you."

This seemed a simple enough first run of the day so they pushed off and went looking. *HMS Skate* proved unmistakeable, the only three funnelled destroyer left in the Navy. She had a gaunt antiquated air about her, low to the water, rust oozing through her battered hull and her tall funnels dominating her. Leaving Punch in charge of *Titch,* Jane went aboard remembering to salute the quarterdeck and again she caused a minor sensation. The Quartermaster looked at her in disbelief, "Here, have you just come out in that little boat? And why are you wearing bell bottoms?"

Jane gave him a wry look. "Because I'm Cox'n of it and work on her all the time. Skirts aren't terribly practical for that sort of work. Watch out Jack, the Wrens are coming."

The Quartermaster shook his head. "I don't believe it."

And round Jane a gathering group of matelots crowded, staring at this apparition. Having got the gangway party to calm down she asked for the Captain. "He's asleep, leave these with me and I'll make sure he gets them."

"I can't do that. I have direct orders to hand them to him personally."

"In which case you'll have to wait; he's left direct orders not to be called until 0800."

"In which case I will wait. Any chance of some scran?"

She was pleased to be handed a plate of sausages and scrambled egg with a huge pot mug of tea. Making sure *Titch* was well secured on the boat boom, Punch joined them and if anything caused a bigger sensation, looking down on the gangway party with a smile of quiet satisfaction. Seated on a ready use locker on the upper deck with morning sun on them and the wind gently ruffling their hair, the two girls kept up a steady banter with the ring of seamen round them. "You're a bit different aren't you?" was the least of the barrage of question fired at them. Again, Jane found that few of them had any real belief in women being able to handle even harbour boats, despite the evidence in front of them. Jane turned the questions back on them, "Don't you mind serving in an old heap like this?"

"Naw, she's a nice old thing and no worse to live in than the Vs and Ws and we get hard liers which helps. And she's a lucky ship; last of her sort and still going strong. You mark my words; this old lady's joss will see her through to the end of the war. You can't do better than sail in a lucky ship."

This chat was interrupted by the Captain's tiger coming aft and saying, "The Captain will see you now, miss." He led Jane to the Captain's sea cabin. Jane had been ready for the full formality of attention and salute but found a bleary eyed lieutenant sitting on his bunk in a dressing gown so came to attention, handed the envelope over and said, "Special orders for you, sir," and made sure that he took hold of them.

"Do I need to sign for them?"

"I wasn't told you had to, only to make sure they were delivered to you personally."

He looked at her, clearly puzzled. "Why are Wrens doing this?"

"We're being tried out as boats crew, sir, and the little skimmer is my boat."

"Good Lord, what will they think of next? You lot should be in the galley."

Jane raised her eyebrows at this but said nothing. "Will that be all, sir?"

"Yes, clear off and don't annoy me."

Jane departed, irritated but also puzzled as to why she was annoying him in the first place. Back at the boats office she got a mild bottle for taking so long.

Life was noticeably quieter in Dover Harbour. With the *Luftwaffe* changing its focus from the convoys and ships to the fighter airfields and major dockyards, Dover was rather left alone while overhead the two air forces fought a fierce war of attrition. Convoys plodded past, occasionally bombed on an opportunist basis, and the Navy kept up its anti-invasion patrols as the German forces built up their strength on the French side. Tension remained high, but for most people life simply went on, albeit with many a glance into the blue sky. Then on 22nd August life in Dover was changed and remained changed for the rest of the war. Suddenly, there was a huge explosion in the town, demolishing several buildings. Out in the Strait, a passing convoy found towering splashes being thrown up round it. It took a little while to work out where these were coming from, but it soon became clear. The Germans had installed giant guns on the cliff tops opposite Dover and for the first time were firing shells able to land on the British mainland. Although Dover was to have its share of air raids in the next few years, it was the shelling which gave it its unique sense of being different and led to its nickname as Hellfire Corner.

* * *

Although it hardly affected Dover, air activity up in the sky was becoming more noticeable with each passing day. Droning wings of bombers passed by at high altitude and for the first time substantial numbers of British fighters were dogfighting with the Germans. The weather remained hot and clear, so the little dots buzzing round were easily seen. Every now and then the battling fighters would come swooping down low over the harbour and sea outside, one in hot pursuit of another and occasionally planes trailing clouds of smoke crashed with a great splash. The Germans had confidently expected to overwhelm the British defences, believing their planes and pilots were better and there were more of them. In fact, there was rough parity between the forces except in one crucial area; Britain was manufacturing many more new fighters than was Germany, so that with equal losses the British were slowly gaining a numerical advantage. The wonderful myth of 'the few' was always half a story. Dowding, carefully hoarding his resources, never sent up as many British fighters as the Luftwaffe sent over. This gave the impression of a brave handful of British pilots taking on German hordes when in fact most of the time he had reserves available.

It only took an airborne German group six minutes to cross the Channel. It took British fighters fifteen minutes to scramble and get up to altitude to take on the advancing Germans. Therefore, early warning was crucial and Britain had the advantage of the chain of radar stations round its coasts. These early and primitive radars were difficult to work and very largely they were under the hands of WAAFs (Women's Auxiliary Air Force). Young women with a lighter touch than most men were found to be well suited to controlling and interpreting the radar screens and this group formed one of the greatest unsung heroes of the whole Battle of Britain. They had to be quick and with experience learnt to make and pass on, early and rapid informed guesses about what their radars were picking up. This gave the British fighters precious extra minutes to get airborne and into position. The demand and stress on these girls was enormous and some paid the ultimate price when their cliff top facilities were bombed, but they remained calm, alert and at their stations throughout. Without this group of talented but unheralded WAAFs the Battle of Britain could easily have been lost.

CHAPTER 15:
Picking Up

By the second half of August the air activity had become intense, with great masses of German aircraft – bombers and fighters – passing over Dover intent on destroying the British fighter airfields. While most bases managed to keep going, the damage and the difficulty was immense and slowly but surely the RAF's ability to put fighters in the air was being strangled. This was a deliberate policy by Goering and had he been able to persist with it the outcome of the Battle of Britain might well have been different. All along, the battle was on a knife-edge and could easily have gone either way but for chance occurrences.

* * *

There was many a dogfight over Dover and from theses, crashing aircraft and parachuting pilots landed in the sea close by. This led to a series of rescues outside Dover Harbour by *Amaryllis* or the picket boat. The girls on *Titch,* kept on harbour duties, could only watch admiringly. Then their chance came; a pilot splashed down only a few hundred yards beyond the harbour mouth. The bigger boats were further out and the whaler tied up alongside, which left only *Titch* close to the airman. Jane looked round, saw no-one else handy and shouted "Come on Punch, it's our turn." They went roaring out of the harbour at full speed and came alongside a broadly grinning young man floating on his Mae West.

"Hello, would you like to be picked up?" enquired Jane politely.

"Good heavens, it's a popsy. What are you doing here?"

"Let's get you in first. Are you all right?"

"Yes, fine, but my plane had its tail shot off."

It took Jane and Punch all their strength to lift him in, but they managed and sitting in the gently rocking boat he smoothed out his moustache, leered at them and repeated.

"What on earth are popsies doing out here?"

"We're boat crew Wrens working in Dover Harbour. I presume you'd like taken ashore?"

"Rather and how about a date?"

"One thing at a time, sunshine. You're obviously not hurt?"

He grinned and shook his head.

"Hang on," shouted Jane and opened *Titch* up to its full twenty knots.

"I say, this is rather fun, isn't it? Fancy being rushed round the oggin by a couple of popsies."

A couple of minutes had them back at the steps and their cheerful young pilot stepped ashore with a farewell wave. The Boats Chief loomed over them ominously.

"You two, in the office now. Boats Officer wants to see you."

Their Boats Officer was standing with cap on so Jane gave him the full salute and report.

"Beacon, you've been warned about heroics. What on earth were you doing rushing outside to pick up a pilot?"

Jane had been expecting some sort of compliment and was a bit taken aback by this.

"We were the closest boat, sir and were on the move so it seemed obvious for us to go."

"That's all very well, but what would have happened if the weather had been bad?"

"*Titch* is actually pretty seaworthy providing you don't rush her, sir and if it had been that bad we wouldn't have gone. But today is harry flatters."

"Yes, quite so. Let me make it quite clear; you are only to go outside as a last resort. You must not go if the weather is force four or more and will not put yourselves at risk in any way. You are not to go more than half a mile to seaward of the pier ends. Is that clear?"

Jane nodded. "Yes sir." There didn't seem any more to say so they saluted and left at his nod of dismissal.

"Oi suppose that could have been worse."

"Probably, Punch. You notice he didn't say we couldn't – only put conditions on it."

"Yes, well they've still not really got us worked out, have they?"

"So much of it is trial and error. They'll learn eventually that we can do anything they can."

"Too right."

The Boats Chief caught up with them. "All right girls, next job is to take some stores round to a motor gunboat. Pick 'em up from Admiralty pier." The stores were for a newly commissioned boat with a Polish crew, who proved to be an enthusiastic lot very keen on a date, which was politely declined.

"Y'know, Punch, if we took up every offer we'd never have a minute to ourselves."

Punch grinned. "There's worse things could happen. Would you rather be left on the shelf?"

"Sometimes, yes. There are times when I could happily do without the men."

"But you're the one who's done it. That doesn't square."

"You might not think so, but believe me, the one follows from the other."

Punch gave her a funny sideways look and picked up her boathook as they arrived back at the steps.

It was a couple of routine days later when their next chance came. On another calm sunny day, an odd-looking parachute came down close behind the Western side of the harbour. Again, *Titch* was the closest boat, so they nipped out and as the pilot landed they pulled alongside him. This one had an orange- topped flying helmet on and was clearly injured. This gave them a problem; how to get him on board without making his injuries worse. He was muttering in German as they brought the boat close alongside. They tried lifting him, but he screamed with pain. Now what were they going to do? Again, it was Punch, the practical seaman who came up with an answer. "Why don't we try using his parachute as a hammock sort of sling, then we can lift him in it without pulling on him."

"Good idea, Punch."

And they worked the parachute round him with some assistance from the airman himself, lifted at each end and managed to get him inboard. It was clear why he screamed when they had pulled; his abdomen was a mass of blood and was evidently badly shot up. Remembering the pilot she had picked coming home from Dunkirk Jane felt round his pockets and sure enough, found a small pistol which she removed and tucked under the foredeck. They roared off at full speed and coming in to the steps frantically called up for an ambulance. This took about fifteen minutes to arrive while the wretched pilot was visibly fading away and was barely alive when they collected him. They heard next day that he had died on the operating table. This bothered Jane. If only they'd been able to summon an ambulance quicker they might have been able to save him. She discussed this with the Boats Chief and they decided to give the boat an Aldis lamp. Punch being a trained signaller was at home with it and it was arranged that if they brought in any more injured airmen she would call the signal station right away and hopefully save a few minutes. Jane quietly decided to keep the German's pistol in case they ever had trouble with any other of his type.

Their next rescue was another British pilot who actually landed inside the detached southern breakwater. Running him in the usual routine started – fancy a date? What are pretty girls like you doing messing about in boats? Punch seemed to enjoy it, but Jane felt irritated by the toplofty superiority of the approach. Growing in confidence, when they saw three parachutes coming down close together close to the Eastern entrance they didn't think twice about it. When they arrived they saw the telltale orange tops to the helmets, but Jane thought, 'All right they might be Boche, but they've still got to be saved.'

It was a mistake. With the three pulled inboard one of them pulled out a pistol, grabbed Punch and held it to her head.

"You, *fraulein,* you go to France." Jane glared back. "No I don't," and she sat down defiantly in the bow of the boat. Another of them moved forward to grab Jane as well, obscuring Punch and her captor. At this point, Jane whipped out the pistol she had taken from the dying German and shot at her aggressor. He screamed and went down in a heap. As he cleared Jane's line of sight she shot again, almost blindly and managed to wing the capturer who went down in a heap as well.

"Punch, grab his gun."

The third German seemed transfixed by the whole performance, staring in wide-eyed horror at his two fallen companions. "Punch, left-hand waist pocket," and with his pistol secured too, they roared back to the steps with Punch frantically signalling for an ambulance, while Jane tried desperately to hide the trembling that ran all through her. Punch was pale white and looked as scared as ever she had. Explaining themselves afterwards was more of a challenge.

"You mean to say you had smuggled a pistol onto your boat and shot two of your captives with it?"

"Well, sir, they weren't really our captives. They were trying to capture us so I prevented it."

"Yes, quite so but you should not have shot them. Meantime hand the guns in and be prepared to account for yourself at a much higher level." For Jane this was not an appealing prospect. 'Not in trouble again' was her primary thought. But the examination proved tame. They were brought before *HMS Wasp's* Captain and Chief Officer Currie; after the usual preliminaries the Captain look intensely at her. "How did you come to have a gun in your boat?"

"Well sir, it goes back to the return from Dunkirk when we rescued one and I discovered that all Hun pilots have a pistol. I managed to get that one's pistol off him, then when we rescued the injured one more recently I took his off him and hid it in the boat. When the three we picked up tried to kidnap us to go to France, I managed to get our pistol out and as he was waving a gun around I felt it was them or us and I simply pulled the trigger. But it all happened so very quickly that really I didn't think about it at all, I reacted."

"Yes, quite so."

Chief Officer Currie interjected, "I didn't know you were a good shot, Beacon."

"Neither did I ma'am. It is the first time I have actually fired a gun of any sort and I'm still not sure how I did it."

The Captain gave Jane a long look, "Shooting Huns is certainly not what we expect from our Wrens." But Jane could see a twinkle in his eye. He turned to Chief Officer Currie and said, "I don't think there is anything much for us to worry about here. Do you?"

"Probably not, sir. If we're going to have Wrens in front line positions, incidents are bound to happen and I suppose Beacon here is exactly the girl to deal with them."

Jane took a risk by cutting in. "Tell me, sir, please, had it been a man in my position would authority have taken such a strong view of the incident?"

The Captain drew a deep breath. "Now that's a good question. Thinking about it, I suppose the answer is no, he'd have been commended for showing initiative and some bravery."

"So, why should a female be treated any differently?"

"Because that's not what we expect of our women."

"At risk of seeming argumentative sir, if this war goes on like it looks as though it will, I suspect that us women are going to be doing a lot more of this sort of thing. This is total war, sir and the old social niceties are being blown away."

"More's the pity, but you may be right."

Chief Officer Currie shook her head slowly with a gentle smile on her face, recognising something familiar. And in effect that was the end of the matter, although another note went into Jane's service record. Jane's reputation as a fighting front line warrior acquired a bit more polish. She was relieved to hear later that both the shot Germans were not seriously injured and would make full recoveries in a prisoner of war camp. Punch and Jane ("Just call us Punch and Judy," remarked Jane) dined out to celebrate and they managed a discreet gulpers session with the other boat crews. Jane's joss held. She was struck by how much she had missed her regular tot of rum; it anesthetised the raw fear that went through her thinking about it afterwards. Again, her capacity to stay cool and act at the time was showing through, the terror only coming later. Which meant the girls were cautious when next they saw a parachute floating down. It was a choppy day but the seas were not so bad that they couldn't venture out.

By early September, the strong sun was easing off and, with more unsettled conditions the girls had changed back into blue shirt and uniform jacket. They had delivered a couple of silent army officers to the batteries on the detached mole when Punch said, "Look, look," and pointed to a parachute descending close outside the harbour. Jane glanced round. The whaler was over with the coastal forces; the picket boat was showing that weakness of all steamers and having a boiler clean. *Amaryllis* was well outside the harbour by some minesweeping trawlers. There could be no argument this time; it was up to *Titch* to collect the pilot.

The girls looked at each other and nodded, Jane gunned the engine and by the time the pilot hit the water *Titch* was less than fifty yards away. He was clearly British, judging by his flying suit, so they were surprised when the big good looking young man they pulled out didn't seem to speak English, but smiled broadly at them. Was he a spy or something?

"Hande hoch," Jane barked at him, while Punch picked up the baton they'd been given as substitute for the pistol.

"Nei, Nei, Polski, Polski." He shouted pointing at himself.

"Oi think he's saying he's a Pole."

"Well, we'll see about that," and Jane went roaring back into the harbour flat out. Running into the steps she called up, "We've got one here who says he's a Pole. Can you get an interpreter?" Jane remembered the coastal forces gun boat with a Polish crew. Fifteen minutes later a Naval Lieutenant with Poland on his shoulder flash appeared and called down to the boat in an unrecognizable language. Their pilot beamed and called back in kind. The Lieutenant nodded happily. "Yes, he's a Polish pilot. Please let him ashore." Their pilot didn't seem to speak much English but gave the girls a big smile and said, "Tank you, tank you," blew them a kiss and disappeared ashore.

Having finished their sandwiches at lunchtime, Jane went ashore to see what the next job was. By the boats office door, her Pole was sitting in the sun. As Jane approached he jumped up.

"Lady, I don't go home to base till tomorrow. You like go out with me tonight?" Jane laughed. There was something very attractive about this good looking young man, from his fiery eyes to his courteous manners and Jane felt an instant attraction. She did a quick calculation; tomorrow was her day off so there was no early rise to cope with. She looked him in the eye, laughed again and said, "Yes, all right. Pick me up at the Wrennery at six thirty." His eyes glowed. There was never any doubt about the purpose of the date and Jane knew it.

CHAPTER 16:
Highs and Lows

"Punch I'm going out with our Pole this evening. I wonder if we can get finished early?" Punch looked sideways at Jane. "You lucky girl. He is rather dishy isn't he?" Jane nodded dreamily and the afternoon passed by in a whizz. Back at the Wrennery in good time, the first hurdle was a quick negotiation with her Quarters Officer, now much more relaxed with Jane.

"Ma'am, an opportunity has come up at short notice and I wondered if I could have a sleeping out pass for tonight?"

This got a slightly jaundiced look from her Quarters Officer. "I won't ask what his name is, but you've only had one late pass since you came back, haven't you? Are you out early tomorrow?"

"No ma'am, I've really been a very good girl. And by chance tomorrow's my day off, so there's no pressure there."

"Oh, all right then." And the precious bit of paper was written out and signed accompanied by a slow shake of the head. With that negotiated she had a quick bath and hair wash, stealing a little extra hot water but too bad, then debated what to wear. It would have to be the black chiffon again. It was starting to get quite well used now, but its shortish full floaty skirt was most convenient for a date like this.

She was startled when he arrived in plain clothes and in an elderly car on the dot of 1830. "I borrow car and clothes from friends on the boat. They help a lot." His hair was combed and he smelt faintly of Eau de Cologne. 'Well, at least he's trying' thought Jane. "Where are we going?"

"I don' know. What you suggest?" His English might be fractured but it was effective. Jane had been doing some rapid thinking. With a car available that country pub was reachable. "I know a nice little pub north of here. Would you like that?"

He smiled, "Yes, I love your pubs." And directed by Jane he went roaring off, pushing the old car to its fairly modest limits. The pub was busy but they got a drink, ordered a meal and settled down in a secluded inglenook. His name was Stefan; the rest was quite unpronounceable. He had been a pilot in the brief unwinnable battle against the German invasion of his homeland and had managed to smuggle himself across Europe, into France and from there to England before the Nazis took France too.

"I ace," he boasted. "Ten kills now an' I hope many more. I hate Germans – I kill 'em, I kill 'em I kill 'em." And he banged the table in time with a fist.

His family were landowners and farmers back in Poland and he pulled out a picture of an ornate country house. "That my home," he said, momentarily sad. Then he stretched out and gently caressed her long scar.

"What happen?"

"Oh, shrapnel at Dunkirk."

"You were at Dunkirk? My God."

So, she had to tell him a bit about it. He laughed, "So, we both heroes and you rescue me. We good together, yes?" And not for the first time Jane found her scar creating a stronger empathy, not the revulsion she had feared.

The meal for the heroes was simple but enjoyable and from there matters got serious. His hand on her knee had progressed to the paradise strip by 'last orders' and they were cuddling up very close. Across his limited English there was a good deal of gentle teasing and laughter. She could see how wound up he was and there was a strange new urge in her own belly. He really was a most attractive young man. This was nothing passive, waiting for the man to make the approach. 'I want you' she thought. 'Now and physically, I want you. What to do next?' Jane decided to take her nerve in both hands and went to the publican. "Any chance of a room for the night?" She was amazed at her own brazenness but the pressure inside pushed her on. The publican gave her a sour smile. "Afraid not, dearie. We're fully booked." Disappointed she reported back to Stefan but he didn't seem bothered. "We have the car. Maybe, that do?"

"It will have to, I suppose!"

He grinned and winked at her, the first drop from the polite and courtly manners he had been showing her all evening, even as his hand had got more intimate. Before they left she retired to the ladies and put her diaphragm in place. Polish passion was one thing; Polish babies quite another.

They found a little country lane and chugged up it into some woodland. The first embrace, awkward across the gear stick, was fiery and from there progress to the back seat was rapid. She could feel his frantic need and felt an answering surge. She whipped her knickers off and murmured, "Oh Stefan, come on." He only lasted a minute the first time, pumping what felt like gallons into her and roaring in incomprehensible Polish. "Two years, two years," he whimpered afterwards and Jane didn't need to ask what he meant. "I do more, I do more," he promised.

"Yes, Stefan, I know. Lots more," and she cuddled his head, which somehow turned into another long kiss. From there the passion was non-stop. In no time they were both naked and exploring each other's bodies; in the narrow confines of the car they discovered a variety of gymnastic new positions. He didn't know that much about female anatomy but was willing to learn and gently murmuring encouragement she helped him to go further. This led him to her most intimate parts and she guided his hand until he got it right. Learning what that could do he repeated it and Jane climaxed explosively again and again. "Jane, Jane, this wonderful new world." And his passion matched hers. Jane laughed and wrapped her arms round him in reply; there didn't seem much need for words. By four in the morning they fell asleep, completely spent, until the sun peeping through the trees at seven thirty brought the entwined bodies back to the surface. Jane would have been willing to accommodate him one last time, but he had nothing left in the tank so they pulled their clothes on and drove back to Dover in a dazed dreamy silence. Arriving, he whispered, "Jane, you change my life." She smiled gently, gave him her address, kissed him once more and shambled into the Wrennery. By good chance there was no-one about so she dumped her clothes, crawled naked under the covers and conked out.

Coming-to in mid afternoon she pulled on her dressing gown and headed for the bathroom. An examination in the mirror was scary – her lips were swollen, her face puffy with dark rings under her eyes. Her body was covered in scratches and little bruises and a big love bite showed vividly on her neck. She was raw between the legs and it felt as though she was walking with her legs several feet apart. She checked in her thoroughly sticky vagina and mercifully her cap was still in place. She thought about douching but decided she wanted to keep something of him inside her for as long as possible. Blessing Sister Donaldson for her skill and advice, Jane drifted back to bed and lay for an hour trying to sort out jumbled thoughts.

Last night had been something quite new. Such passion and fierce lust were on a different scale to Jean-Pierre's skilled but gentle ministrations or the dreadful PTI's selfish banging. What was special – and a really surprising revelation - was how aggressively she had met his fire. Being an equally active partner as much as a receiver was a new experience and the remembrance warmed through her. She smiled quietly to herself, thinking about it all. Then that nagging irritating moralist voice popped into the back of her brain.

'Really,' it said,' less than twelve hours from fishing him out of the oggin to opening your legs for him. What were you thinking of? That really is the height of sluttishness. All right, you've always been an impulsive creature, but you should be ashamed of yourself for this performance. You were like a wild animal.'

'I don't know' came the reply from the front of her brain, 'perhaps that's right but, but...it felt right from the first time we looked at each other and knew we were going to do it. If I'm going to behave like a slut, that's the way to do it.' Yet the confusion remained in her mind - if that was being a loose woman then it was rather wonderful - but at the same time she knew she shouldn't be doing it, she really shouldn't. 'Oh well,' she thought, 'I don't suppose there's any reconciling those so being careful is the only answer. But last night? So much for being careful there.' As she drifted off to sleep again her last thought was that she had had a Frenchman, a Welshman and now a Pole. I wonder what an Englishman would be like?

Her alarm's summons at six the next morning was not welcome. Starving, she demolished three bowls of cereal instead of her usual one. Punch, who although still *intacto* knew the score, gave Jane's ragged appearance a long silent look, smiled and muttered "filthy stopout". Jane had wrapped a scarf round her neck and prayed that no-one would object to its non-uniform presence. The day proved routine which was just as well given her dazed state. She handed control of *Titch* to Punch, and noted that the big girl was as at ease on the controls as she was at anything else in a boat. 'Interesting' thought Jane 'We know who Cox'n number two will be.' Punch said very little, just gave Jane ironic glances from time to time. A day in the fresh air and Jane was feeling better and a good night's sleep left her more or less back in normal condition, give or take a few scratches, bruises and the livid love bite. The events of that night kept coming back to haunt her. She had discovered a whole new part of herself, something she had never even suspected she had. Sex with Jean-Pierre had been delightful and energetic enough when he got her going but that was the point; it was something that was done to her. The night with Stefan had been very different and she was amazed at her lust fuelled ferocious equality in their sex. Driving round the harbour she had to shake herself to concentrate on the current job and not go off into a daze. Punch quietly held it all together with no sign of annoyance at her crewmate's state.

After several days of this, Jane was recovering her equilibrium and getting actively involved in the job again. They were out on a routine trip to the South Breakwater batteries, delivering the mail and some small stores, when yet another dogfight brewed up overhead. They were less frequent now and didn't seem to involve the mass of aeroplanes that they had, but were still spectacular affairs in clear blue sky.

As the fight went on several planes crashed spectacularly, diving into the sea at great speed trailing clouds of smoke. Then a Hurricane came down at a shallow angle, heading for the harbour mouth almost as though trying to dock. Clouds of smoke trailed out behind it. It pancaked onto the sea and didn't sink, only a few hundred yards from the harbour entrance. Jane didn't even look at Punch she swung *Titch* and went roaring out at full speed. The plane was still afloat when they got to it nose down and flames licking all round its cockpit where they saw the pilot slumped in his seat. Mercifully, his canopy was slid back. Jane manoeuvred *Titch* in behind the wing and grabbing a painter jumped onto the wing and from there up to the cockpit. Punch followed. The pilot was obviously badly injured, but still alive. The two girls struggled to release his safety harness and lift him out, beating back the flames with their feet. They slid him onto the wing then, with one huge heave got him over *Titch's* bulwark and laid on the bottom boards. Thirty seconds later the Hurricane stood on its nose and quietly slid beneath the sea with a hissing as the flames went out. The pilot's clothes were still smouldering and he was severely burnt. Jane released his oxygen mask and looked at the burnt pulpy mass that had been his face. There was something familiar about the nose.

"Horace! Oh no, Horace!" she wailed.

He briefly opened his eyes, tried to smile and said, "Hello Jane. Tell mummy I love her." Then he slumped dead in her arms. One less of *Osprey's* crew. Jane took his hand in some sort of gesture of farewell, but to her horror it came off in hers, the blackened claw coming adrift from the remains of the arm it had been attached to. Jane stared at it stupidly for an eternity and then suddenly dropped it in revulsion. Briefly, she stared ahead blankly, then shook herself. Punch meantime had taken the controls and was roaring into the harbour. "No need to panic for an ambulance, Punch. I'll take the boat – you signal one cadaver to land."

"You knew him?"

"Yes." The flat monosyllable was all Jane could manage. After the recent emotional high Jane was having extreme difficulty coping with the low she was now feeling. She sat down that night to write.

'Dear Mrs Horan,

This is the most painful letter I have ever had to write. In our work I have rescued a few ditched airmen but this is the first time it has been someone I knew. We got Horace out and if nothing else it will be possible for him to be returned to you, which I hope will help a little. His last words were, "Tell mummy I love her." Horace has been a valued part of my life too, since early childhood, but nothing can replace the bond between mother and child and I can assure you that Horace felt it even as he left us.

At least he died in the arms of someone he knew and who cared for him, if that is any comfort to you at all.

With sad love

Jane Beacon

Leading Wren, Dover Harbour

She went to bed and wept silently for some time. Horace had never been more than one of her chums, one of the longstanding gang of friends and every bit as keen a sailor. But that night the nightmares had a fresh twist, of detached hands waving around to join the faces, which came back with a vengeance. Her cabin mates had to call the night doctor who in turn called a senior doctor who by chance was Jamie, but even he could only sedate her and wait for the howling to stop. Next day she was even more washed out than she had been so recently. Later that morning they were summoned to the Boats Officer's lair.

"We watched you through the binoculars yesterday. That was a remarkably brave thing you two did. But Beacon, you needn't think it will add to your tally of medals. The best we'll do is another Mentioned in Despatches. And a first one for you, Johnson."

Jane had to remind herself that Punch was called Johnson.

"I'm sorry sir, what is this about medals? I know nothing about that."

He looked amazed. "You mean you've not been told?"

Jane could only shake her head.

"Oh well, it's not for me to say anything. You'll find out. Now you can go back to work. I think the Admiral wants a trip with you."

Jane smile broadly while saluting Rear-Admiral Rodmayne on board. He wanted to look at the harbour from seaward for reasons of his own, so they butted out into a short choppy sea that was not kind to *Titch*. Observations completed, they ran back and were instructed to tie up to one of the cylindrical mooring buoys on the trots, now rarely used.

"Jane, I've been meaning to speak to you for a while. Congratulations on your progress, you really are doing remarkably well. I watched your rescue the other day and was most impressed."

Jane smiled.

"Dealing with the three Germans was scarier, sir. I don't think I like shooting people. But at least I didn't kill them."

He sighed. "Yes, three more mouths to feed. But that's not why I'm here. I wanted to tell you I'm being appointed to the Eastern Mediterranean next month and after that you're on your own. I've had a chat with your Director about you and she has someone on her staff keeping an eye on you, so with any luck the wolves at the Admiralty won't get you. But you will have to be very careful not to give them any excuses. No more dodgy Frenchmen."

Jane gulped, a guilty start that set her blushing despite her attempts to look nonchalant. He looked at her keenly. "Not again Jane? Hopefully not in a ship?"

Jane didn't know whether to nod, shake her head or just hope the sea would swallow her up. At least she could blurt out "Not in a ship, sir."

Punch snorted.

"Well, that's some relief, anyway. Good luck and now let's get going."

"Thank you sir and good luck to you too. The Eastern Med's quite a hot place."

His eyes gleamed. "Yes, some proper seagoing and a chance for some action."

When they came in at the end of their day there was a letter for Jane in an unfamiliar hand. Curious, she opened it.

"*My dear Jane,*

Your sad letter reached me the day after I got the telegram about Horace. While I can only say as a mother that I am devastated by his loss, your letter brought more comfort to me than you can imagine. To know that he was not alone at the end, that he died in the arms of someone who cared for him, gives me immense relief and strength and I thank you a million times for writing to me. Please call on me when next you are on leave.

With thanks and love

Amelia Horan

An upsurge of emotion swept over her again and she sat on her bunk quietly weeping for some time.

CHAPTER 17:
The Complexities of Life

The constant invasion scares in Dover kept everyone on edge, but invasion scares take many forms and Jane was totally unprepared for her next one. Six excitable Polish seamen stormed into the front hall of the Wrennery demanding to see the "Beautiful Beacon".

"We from motor gun boat, good friend of Stefan...." and some impossible Polish surname. "He tell us what beautiful girl you are. We want take you out too."

Jane sensed a trap here. They were lively and attractive young men, but what did they mean by 'Take you out, too?'

"Boys, that's very kind of you but being with Stefan was very special and not something I will repeat. I don't mind a drink with you but that's all, do you understand?"

They looked at each other, "All right, you come tonight?"

Which is how she found herself in a pub with a pint of beer and six very lively Poles. She was fairly expert at nursing a pint by now so was able to stay reasonably sober. They told her tales of a happy land settled in rural peace, of their homes and families and dogs and how much they missed them. "We beat Hitler, you see, then we go home again." And if there were perhaps more hands patting her knee than were strictly necessary they seemed happy to talk nostalgically and want a pretty girl to listen to them. But maybe, not all. A tall darkly bearded killick suddenly looked at her and said, "You very good to Stefan. You be good to me too?"

'Oh, Lordie' thought Jane 'this was bound to happen,' and felt acutely embarrassed. She shook her head, suspecting there was no point in being coy about it. "No, I won't. What I did with Stefan was very special and not for anyone else. I'm happy to have a beer with you but that is all. Do you understand? I don't know what Stefan told you but believe me, I don't normally do that sort of thing."

"Ah, but Beacon, you lovely girl. Why keep it to yourself? You strong enough to do all of us."

Jane gulped. A reputation like that was seriously bad news. "Please understand me, that was different and I'm not doing it again. How can I explain this? There was a special magic with Stefan and me, but magic like that can't be transferred so I'm afraid you are out of luck."

They were all listening intently to this exchange and a murmour of disappointment went round them. They had obviously expected more.

"We got good money, look," and the killick waved some banknotes at her. This was even worse and she coloured deeply. "Please, please, understand me, you might not believe it but really I'm not that sort of girl." Both knees now had hands on them. "Please, boys, I don't want to upset you, but really I'm not available and I will not be pleasing any of you more than by being here. You must understand that."

Panic was beginning to rise in her throat and she looked for the exits. But abruptly they pulled back. "All right, Stefan lucky man. But we like you for mascot. Maybe you visit our boat sometime?"

"Provided it's a properly organised party and I can bring a few friends."

There was a rumble of agreement. Drinks finished, they all moved off and escorted Jane back to the Wrennery. Thinking about it later she had a feeling of a lucky escape and of worry about how much Stefan had told them. Why did men have to boast about it? On the other hand, once this lot had accepted that they weren't going to get anything from her they had behaved in a decent way. If kept within bounds, they could be a delightful lot, but that had been too close for comfort.

Eating their lunch sandwiches the next day in the boat, gently bobbing at a mooring buoy out in the trots, Punch gave Jane a sideways look and casually asked, "You been at it again? I saw those Poles last night."

Jane shook her head vehemently. "No I haven't. They fancied the idea but I was having none of it. Punch, I don't spread it around, really I don't."

"Only when it suits you, you mean."

"Oh, this is terrible. Why have you all got me fixed for a slut? I'm not really, I'm not."

Punch snorted; this appeared to be a speciality of hers.

"As far as I know, you're the most active girl in the Wrennery. Certainly that's how the girls see you. Oi've seen a lot of funny things go on in the docks and I know the signs. You have a quite different attitude to the others and maybe that's why you're seen differently. Y'know, your attitude is much more like the good time girls I've seen round the dockside pubs. Like them you don't seem to care one way or the other. And look at the state of you when you came back from that Pole. Talk about a wreck." For Punch this was a long speech.

Jane was getting seriously worried. Punch had said very little about their relationship, seemingly happy simply to be in the boat, but this smelt bad. "Do you mind all this? Y'know, being crew hand in the boat when you could so obviously be in charge yourself and having to put up with my other stuff?"

"No Jane, Oi don't. You don't know how strong you are and I'm happy with that. Sometimes I think you're a bit silly, but that's nothing compared with all the good stuff. No, Jane I'm quite happy to tag along with you and help out when I can. Don't worry."

"Well I hope so. I sure as hell don't want to lose you."

"No chance." And Punch grinned, an ironic but face splitting grin that said more than a hundred words. Jane couldn't resist giving the big girl a hug and struggled to keep the tears out of her eyes. The thought that she might lose Punch had suddenly appalled her. Somehow Punch's calm through the recent highs and lows had been wonderfully stabilising in an unstated way. Jane might not be – or want to be – Punch's oppo, but as her first line of support she was vital. Sandwiches finished, Jane muttered, "I suppose we'd better find out what marvellous job chiefie has got lined up for us. Let's go." It was likely to be routine.

The note on the board was peremptory. "*Leading Wren Beacon report to OiC's office 0900 tomorrow.*" Quarters Officer emerged and saw Jane picking up the note. "Ah, Beacon, you've seen it, don't be late."

"What have I done this time?" wailed Jane.

"Nothing new, I don't think. I can't say more but I don't think it is bad news."

Next day Jane in best uniform presented herself at ten to nine and waited. Summoned to the presence she was surprised to find Chief Officer Currie in a sunny mood. "Well now, Beacon, your exploits have caught up with you. Here's a letter from headquarters. Sit down and read it please."

Please advise Leading Wren Jane Beacon WRNS that His Majesty the King, on the advice of the medals committee is pleased to agree to the request of the Army to award Miss Beacon the Medal for Distinguished Conduct in the Field in recognition of her services to the Army on the beaches of Dunkirk. Of her many exploits, her extraction of the rear guard under fire has been particularly mentioned.

His Majesty is also pleased to accept the advice of Their Lordships of the Admiralty who feel obliged to follow suit and has therefore awarded Miss Beacon the Conspicuous Gallantry Medal.

Miss Beacon will receive these awards from His Majesty at Buckingham Palace on Friday 27th September, the ceremony to commence at 1100 am. Please instruct Miss Beacon to be at the Palace no later than 1030.

Both the French and Belgian free authorities in London also wish to make awards to Miss Beacon and she is commanded to attend at the French Legation in London at 1600 the same day. Unrestricted permission is granted to Leading Wren Beacon to wear these foreign decorations.

May we extend our congratulations to Leading Wren Beacon for these awards. She is entitled to seven days' award leave after the ceremony.

Vera Laughton Matthews
Director
Women's Royal Naval Service

Jane looked at the letter in disbelief. Summoned to the Palace? Receive medals? Subsequently, attend at the French Legation? The thought terrified her. Her manners had been drummed into her long since and she could curtsey with the best of them, but actually going and standing before the King? Scary. This must be what people had been hinting at and others had known about for some time. She felt a mild resentment at it being known elsewhere while she had been kept in the dark, but did that really matter? Probably not. She looked up at Chief Officer Currie who was smiling broadly. "May I be the first to congratulate you, Beacon? I'm not sure their Lordships are entirely happy about this, but I do know the pressure from the Army has been huge."

"Thank you, Ma'am. This will take a little while to sink in. Do I need to do anything now?"

"No Beacon, simply get yourself ready to look your best on the day. You'll be in uniform, of course. Come and see me again about practicalities in a few days' time and there will be more advice on how you comport yourself. Here is a copy of the letter for you."

And with that Jane got the nod of dismissal. She floated out of the office on a little cloud, feet not seeming to touch the ground.

Back in her cabin, she looked at the calendar. Today was the eighteenth. The summons was for the twenty-seventh and she could bring one guest with her. Who would that be? It was probably too late for any of her family to be able to come up and she had no particular friend to share it with. For a moment, she toyed with the idea of inviting her godfather but decided that was probably a bit much. She would have to go on her own. With the time the letter had taken to get to her, there was little left to get organised. She would need leave from the Boats Officer and to see her Chief Officer again similarly. How long? The letter talked of leave after the ceremony, which might give her a chance to go home for a few days, which would be nice. Sitting in her cabin that evening she showed the letter to Jo who squealed with delight. "Jane! That's marvellous! I've heard the stories but you must have done even more to get that collection. I'd no idea I was sharing a cabin with such a heroine." And that hero worship, which Jane found so uncomfortable, shone in Jo's eyes.

Buoyed up though she was by this news, there was a job to be done and next day she was out on the water as usual. Punch was pleased for her commenting, "Now you know why I'm happy to stay with you."

Did she know? Jane debated why her getting recognition for what she'd done alone at Dunkirk should make Punch want to stay with her, but that young woman tended to mean what she said so it must satisfy at some level. But level-headed Punch showed no more excitement and they got on with a very routine day. Mail to the batteries on the breakwater, stores to a visiting destroyer, then its Captain to run ashore, an RAF officer to be shown where the defensive guns were placed, a quick dash with orders out to a minesweeping trawler which came-to off the harbour mouth and a period in mid-afternoon when they lay at the boat steps waiting for orders, all were dull, but necessary. For Jane, this stuff was getting boring after the intense adrenalin rushes of recent times, but at least it kept her in the boats. Leave was something to look forward to; she realised that apart from her convalescent period she had'd no time off since last Christmas and wasn't even sure what her entitlement was.

The Boats Officer, who already knew what was coming, was relaxed about releasing Jane for a couple of weeks. Punch could drive the boat – he had already noted how competent she was in boat handling – and he would make sure the same reliable AB as had been with Jane early on, would be assigned to *Titch* with Punch. That dealt with, she made an appointment to see her Chief Officer again. Coming in, Jane, as ever, came to attention, saluted and reported. Chief Officer Currie looked at her quizzically, "Well Beacon, it makes a nice change to have you here for good reasons. First of all, may I repeat my congratulations. This clutch of medals puts you in a different league from any other Wren. But remember you are still only a Leading Wren and do not go getting ideas. You argue quite enough as it is."

Jane drew breath to protest about this but Chief Officer Currie was a forceful lady when necessary and held up a peremptory hand. "There you go again, Beacon. I've never known a girl like you for arguing. I'm sure when you appear before the King you'll tell him he's got it wrong. But I didn't make the appointment to argue with you, so kindly be quiet for ten seconds at least. Now, headquarters have ordained that you should have hotel accommodation for three nights during the ceremony period so that is being arranged at the Charing Cross Hotel where we have rooms, usually for officers. They want to see you at headquarters the day after you receive your medals and an appointment with the Director has been made for 1030. Do not be late. You then have a week's leave, so I presume you will go home?"

Jane nodded. "Yes ma'am, I have had virtually no ordinary leave since I started and I must say the thought of a week off is quite appealing."

This got a slightly bleak smile from her Chief Officer. "Well, we're here for a purpose so you can't expect too much leeway but coming down from the experiences you have had can't be easy, so a short break will probably do you good. After your leave you will come back here but headquarters have ideas that they want to discuss with you when you go to see them which may subsequently change things. In the meantime, everything is organised so may I add my best wishes."

"Well, thank you ma'am. It is all a bit much to take in and I'm still not sure I deserve it, but who am I to say no?"

"Who indeed?" And on getting the nod of dismissal Jane saluted, about turned and sailed out of the office. Her nervousness was getting stronger.

She wrote home with the news, then to the names on the list from Probationer Course and received replies varying from ecstatic to envious. Alicia loved her despatch riding and was based in London and Jane must have dinner with her while in town; it would be good to catch up. Camilla was at Greenwich on the officers' training course prior to becoming a Cipher Officer. Fiona, whose written English took away the strong accent and was markedly fluent, was doing a visual signaller course and enjoying life. She had heard from Dora who was flourishing in the Wrens after her difficult beginning and was now a leading Wren in the regulating branch. 'She should be ideal for the job' was Fiona's gently ironic comment. The only odd letter came from Merle. She was a third officer now working at headquarters and doing well; the WRNS was helping her with her solicitor's training. She then went on to say that 'she was delighted things were working out as planned for Jane and that the Admiralty opposition had relented sufficiently for the awards to be made'. There was an implication of insider knowledge there that Jane didn't understand but had no time to investigate. The other person to tell had to be Stan. He received the news philosophically. "Ee, lass, it's no more than you deserve and it was obvious from when you blew your top under the gash chute that you were going to be a bit different. Congratulations. I got my DSM for an action on the China Station but now you're ahead of me." And when the news went round the rest of the boat crews there was a gulpers session led by Nobby that left Jane very unsteady. But her joss held and she was able to totter to her bunk unseen. At least it eased the strong sense of terror which was gripping her.

There was one other letter for Jane at this time. Addressed to 'The Beautiful Beacon' in a foreign hand, it proved to be from Stefan who clearly had received some help in composing it. Mainly it raved about how wonderful their night together had been and how he was forever dreaming of her and please could he have a picture? Now, he had more than his hatred of Germans to live for and when were they going to meet again? This put Jane in a bit of a quandary. Like Jean-Pierre before, she had rather consigned Stefan to happy memories and she remembered all too vividly what had happened when she let Jean-Pierre back into her life briefly. What should she do about Stefan? He was a nice guy and deserved to be treated kindly. Well, she didn't have any photos of herself to hand so asked Jo if any of her spreading clan were photographers and wasn't surprised to be told "yes". Making sure the shots were mainly of her good side and that the scar was only glimpsed, she got a set of good studio pictures taken in uniform and in mufti. She sent one off to Stefan along with a letter making friendly noises but without any promises of meeting again.

* * *

Meanwhile, the planes seemed to have gone away from Dover. It was now mid-September 1940 and although they knew nothing about it at Dover, Germany had changed tactics. In a fit of rage at Berlin being bombed by the British, Hitler ordered the Luftwaffe to change to bombing London. It was a catastrophic mistake. Although they did not know it, the German bombers were near to bringing Britain's fighter command to a halt with its campaign of constantly attacking the airfields. Two more weeks would have done it. Yet again, Britain survived by chance and the slenderest of threads.

Down in Dover, several times there were hysterical active invasion alerts, as though the armada of barges and small ships had put out, but each time it proved to be a false alarm. They were very conscious in Dover that they were on the front line, that if the Wehrmacht just twenty-one miles away did take its life in its hands and sail, it could be in Dover in a matter of hours. But nobody flinched, the population took some pride in staying put, refusing to be frightened out or cowed by the heavy, if intermittent, shelling which was now becoming part of life. Against this backdrop everyday life went on.

And by mid-September the German war machine was coming to accept that it was not beating Britain in the air. There was never the clear-cut aerial victory that some propaganda claimed; the Luftwaffe was never defeated, but neither was the RAF and that was the point. Simply by remaining a fighting force in being it denied the Germans unhindered use of the air. It was this fact that the RAF was not beaten and remained as fierce a threat as ever, which was the critical factor. As the Blitz showed, German aircraft were still able to roam over Britain, especially at night, but Goering's promise that he would sweep British planes from the sky proved to be no more than bluster.

Both sides knew that control of the air was crucial for the German invasion plan to succeed. But the reasons for this were more complex than simple Lords of the Air trumpeting. The German invasion force of canal barges and small boats had to be protected from the Royal Navy if it was to get across the Channel. After its recent mauling off North Norway the Kreigsmarine was in no position to offer this protection, so it was up to the Luftwaffe to keep the Royal Navy at bay. It could only do that if it had control of the skies. The Royal Navy would have been duty bound to throw everything it had at the invasion force and would have done so unhesitatingly whatever the odds. With control of the air, the Luftwaffe would simply have bombed the British warships to the seabed and the barges could have crossed unhindered. Without that air domination, the Luftwaffe would still have been a nuisance and sunk some British ships, but could not have prevented the Navy's big guns from getting at and wreaking havoc in the fleet of thin-skinned barges carrying the cream of the Wehrmacht to their doom. Even a destroyer's 4.5 inch guns could sink a barge with one shell. There is no doubt that by surviving and remaining a potent threat, the Royal Air Force prevented the invasion of Britain, but it was more of a complex joint services matter than is sometimes credited.

From late September onwards the threat of invasion slowly faded. In fact, Hitler was steadily withdrawing the invasion force through the Autumn his mind turning to the East and especially to invading Russia. But it took some time for that message to filter down through the British population and it was 1941 before the threat of invasion was consigned to history.

PART FIVE:

LONDON

CHAPTER 18:
Before the King

In the rest of the brief intervening time before going up to London Jane made sure her best uniform was dry-cleaned and as smart as possible. She had her shoes polished until she could see her face in them and bought a couple of pairs of best black silk stockings. She had read that the Service's Chief Commandant, Princess Marina, Duchess of Kent, always carried a spare pair of stockings whenever she went in uniform and this struck Jane as a very sensible idea so two pairs were needed. In doing this, she wrote out cheques on her nice quietly enlarging bank account, courtesy of her father and was startled to discover that a Coutts & Co cheque was very well received. It had not occurred to her that it was anything more than a bank account until she produced the first cheque and the people behind the counter suddenly turned very obsequious indeed. With fifty pounds in the account she felt rich. Her daily life was simple and dominated by the Wrens, which meant that she had little need to spend much more than the pittance her pay produced each week. Faced with spending a little more, she found she was well served and what she needed for purchases barely dented the funds in her bank account.

Looking at her uniform she debated which hat to wear. On returning from convalescent leave she had been issued with a new one and told the old was a disgrace, but so much life and adventure was wrapped up in it that she couldn't bear to throw it away and she wore it whenever she could. Might she get away with wearing it to the investiture? With a day to go until she left Dover she was a bag of nerves, even snarling at Punch who only lifted an eyebrow as comment. At the end of that day Punch suddenly gave her a hug and murmured, "Don't worry, you'll be fine when you get there." From this undemonstrative young lady it was comfort indeed. Her train wasn't due to leave till 1300 next day leaving her ample time to pack in the morning but, tense as anything, she went through the contents of her case for the umpteenth time that night. Feeling more like a condemned person than one going to be congratulated, she was half an hour early for her train but even then only just managed to bag a seat.

Having checked in at the hotel, she contemplated what to wear for dinner with Alicia, settling in the end for her best doeskin uniform on the grounds that it could do with a preliminary try-out before the big day tomorrow. The Cafe Royal was one of those ornate Victorian restaurants, which had not changed in fifty years, but had a polished comfort to it. Jane came in looking for other Wrens, but was startled by a voice behind her saying "Hello, Jane."

"Alicia! Lovely to see you."

Then, from behind a potted palm stepped Camilla, grinning gently. "Well, I'll be damned, you too! What a re-union." Meeting Camilla as well was an unexpected bonus, despite Jane having had misgivings about her on the Pro Course. Camilla was as small and dainty as ever, dressed in a pale blue silk sheath that made Jane feel a bit like a uniformed giraffe. Alicia likewise, was in plain clothes, in her case a smart linen suit in greys and cream with a rather fetching small-brimmed bowler hat on the back of her head.

Camilla looked appraisingly at Jane's white lanyard, tucked under her jacket collar and tight across her front. "It looks very business like, but why?"

"Oh, we need to have a knife on a lanyard in the boat and it's become a bit of a badge of office since I started doing it on the beach at Dunkirk."

"Ah, yes, the beaches of Dunkirk. Rumour has it you're in for a clutch of medals. Is it true?"

"More or less, yes. I think the Army's really driving it, given that the Admiralty don't think much of me."

"Don't they? Why ever not?"

"Something to do with me pinching a boat and disobeying orders and being where they didn't think a female should be. Not what the Navy expects from its ladies. There's someone high up there who wants me chucked out completely. I'd like to get hold of him."

"He'd get a surprise or two if you did."

Jane smiled gently at the thought.

They ordered a round of pink gins and fell to catching up. Camilla, settling demurely on the edge of her seat said, "Jane darling, I think I owe you an apology. When I got home from Probationer Course I asked my father about yours. I had no idea he was quite so eminent a physician. You should have said."

Jane waved away the idea. "Oh, he's certainly well known and people come to him from all across England, but I didn't think he was that special. And anyway, I am trying to live my own life, not live in his shadow."

"You're certainly doing that."

"How's the officer course going?"

"Greenwich really is the most divine place," enthused Camilla. "The painted hall has to be the most gorgeous dining hall there is and the staff are so skilled. So far we've not had any real problems with the bombing, although sleeping down in the cellars isn't much fun. But I suppose we have to do it." And she pulled her mouth down in mock complaint.

Jane turned to Alicia, "Tell me, is despatch riding as exciting as it's made out to be?"

"Sometimes yes, when you're trying to get urgent messages through blitzed streets and the ARP wardens don't want to let you through. But so far I've not had any major excitements. But do tell us all about boating. Can we get into it too?"

"Well, Camilla couldn't because it's ratings only to match how the Navy does it. I still think that's silly, but our own people don't seem to want to challenge it so we're stuck with it. But aren't you the same at despatch riding?"

"Yes, except for a few administration officers."

"Admin officers, bah. Full of their own importance and not much else."

Camilla snorted with laughter in a gentle ladylike way. "I'm finding it awfully strange changing from being a bolshie Wren to being officer class."

"You, Camilla? Bolshie? I'd never have thought it."

"Well, I did give my last boss a bit of a hard time of it when she wouldn't give me time off to come up to town. Poor dear. She didn't know what to do with me when I really got difficult. I think she recommended me for officer to get rid of me." She changed the subject. "Tell me, Jane, how is your bottom?"

"Oh, it will never be beautiful again with stripy scars across it, but it's no problem to live with; no pain or difficulty."

"Oh dear, without a beautiful bottom how will you ever get a man?"

"So far that's not been a problem, but doubtless it will one of these days."

"You mean you've got a man, anyway?"

Jane blushed. "Not now, but one did want to know about them and it was a bit difficult to explain."

"Jane dear, you've been at it again; haven't you?"

"Not really, he got a little close and surprised."

"I'll bet he was surprised. How did you explain that away?"

"Didn't try, actually. Got him interested in something else and he forgot about my stripes."

All three girls dissolved into fits of giggles.

"Did you hear that Mrs Brown was up to her tricks again in the ATS and ended up in deep trouble? Apparently, she ordered a caning for a girl who ran away and when the girl complained to the Police, they arrested our dear Mrs B and gave her a hard time of it. Now she's in the Land Army, digging potatoes."

"Can't have much further to drop. I wonder if her farmer is giving her a bit of it?"

"Would do her good." They roared with very unladylike whoops of glee.

They raised their glasses. "Here's to defying the enemy and even more to our superiors, may the two meet on Tuesday."

"I reckon our Wren seniors could scare Hitler into submission in a week. Shall we send a group of them to Berlin?"

They chatted away non-stop through the meal, ignoring an air raid warning, as did most of the other diners. It was Camilla who asked, "What do you think of the sinking of the *City of Benares*? Those poor kids; I think it was about eighty that were lost?"

"It looks like the whole evacuation programme will be stopped now. We can't go on sending children to be drowned in the Atlantic."

Jane was listening intently. Down in Dover, wrapped up in her own affairs she had read about the sinking a week before, but had dismissed it as one more merchant ship torpedoed. "Was it so terrible?"

"Well, only because of all the children who were lost, but imagine what their parents must be feeling."

"Yes, pretty horrible. Did I read that there's a demand for the U-boat captain to be declared a war criminal?"

"There's certainly plenty of popular indignation, but also a feeling that he was simply doing his job. He couldn't have known there were children aboard the ship."

They debated for ten minutes whether all U-boat captains should be called war criminals, but then what about our own submarine skippers? It was a difficult one with no obvious conclusion. Later, there was a gentle argument about who was going to pay the bill so they settled for each paying a third and by the time they parted Jane was much more relaxed. They promised to meet again in a few months' time and to keep in touch meantime. Jane went back to the hotel feeling rather better about Camilla.

Investiture day loomed and Jane was up early. She managed a leisurely bath, selected a new pair of stockings, collected her highly polished shoes from outside her room door and dressed. It was all she could manage to eat some toast, the butterflies in her stomach warring with the constriction in her throat. The taxi she had ordered was on time and she was deposited outside the Palace at ten o'clock prompt. It took some enquiring around to find the right entrance, skirting the bomb damage from earlier in the week. The anteroom where people were being marshalled was already well filled. She was the only female and the only rating there but there were plenty of tense looking officers from all three services, plus a couple of firemen. Some sat, some milled around, one who lit a cigarette was sharply told to put it out. Looking round Jane thought that going into battle was probably less stressful than this waiting. At a quarter to eleven, they were addressed by a lordly gentleman in knee breeches and some sort of full regalia, which Jane didn't recognise. Then, they were led to the entrance of a ground floor semi State Room being used in preference to the ballroom, this being considered too dangerous. The King arrived escorted by two

Ghurkha soldiers as always. The Guards orchestra played the National Anthem. The King invited the assembly to sit and the first recipient, a very senior Naval Officer, stepped forward.

Jane was number eight in the queue of thirty-two which meant her turn came soon enough. When number seven went in, she quickly whipped off her new hat and on went the battle scarred number, stuffing her new one in a pocket. An equerry tried to protest, but she held a finger to her mouth to indicate to him to "shut up". As she stepped in, absolutely terrified, the orchestra changed to a selection from *HMS Pinafore*, starting with *I'm Little Buttercup*, a reference that Jane recognised and smiled at inwardly. They had evidently been waiting for her. She had been briefed to curtsey, not salute, three steps back from the King, then step up to one pace away. The Lord Chamberlain, at the King's elbow, announced, "Leading Wren Jane Beacon, decorated for bravery on the beaches of Dunkirk." As Jane stood rigidly to attention the King smiled. "Ah, Beacon, I am delighted to be making these awards to you." He pinned on first the Army Distinguished Conduct Medal, then the Navy Conspicuous Gallantry Medal. Jane was ready to take three steps back, curtsey again and exit to the right, but the King spoke to her again. "I have read the citations for your awards and I am very impressed by your bravery. Were you not terrified?"

"Not really, sire. I was so busy getting on with it that fear didn't occur to me. If anything some of the people I rescued were more scary than the Stukas."

The King smiled broadly. "The whole story is quite intriguing. Mr Churchill and I were so taken by it that we felt some further mark of esteem from us might be in order, although negotiating it with the Navy was not easy. However, Mr Churchill prevailed and therefore, I have pleasure in investing you as a Member of the Order of the British Empire in the Military Division." And he pinned on another medal above the other two. Jane was totally taken aback by this. She flushed and because he evidently expected a response said, "Well, thank you, sire. This is an exceptional honour, which I didn't expect."

He smiled, shook her hand and nodded slightly so she took the requisite three steps back, curtseyed low again and exited to the back of the room to find a gilt and red velvet seat. Once the ceremony was over, the King retired. Although Jane did not know it at the time, this was the last investiture at Buckingham Palace for some time because of the bombing and she had been the first rating to get her awards at the Palace.

Released, people mingled in the courtyard. Most had a family member or a friend with them, which rather left Jane on her own so she wasn't sorry when a tall good-looking Lieutenant-Commander singled her out. "Hello, how nice to meet you again."

Jane looked puzzled. "Well yes, but again?"

"You don't remember me, do you?" he said with a teasing laugh.

"I'm sorry, I can't say I do."

"Dunkirk? Remember a sinking burning old V class destroyer? You rescued people from the foc'sle head?"

"Oh, I remember that all right. Those flames were fierce."

"Well, I was the two and a half you rescued."

"No, I don't believe it. How many injured people were there?"

He smiled gently at her little trap. "Two: the upper deck buffer with a broken leg and an AB with shrapnel wounds. Or I suppose three if you include me. We lowered them down in a bosun's chair and I came last, sliding down a rope."

"Good Lord, so it was you! Well I never! I wouldn't have recognised you. I must say you do look a bit different today, but it's nice to see you well again. How's your leg?"

"Oh, fine. It was only a flesh wound. But your face suffered, didn't it?"

"I'm afraid so, although they tell me it will calm down more in time. Was it you who recommended me for a medal, then?"

He laughed. "Not entirely. My Report of Proceedings did praise you highly, but a humble two and a half can't usually put people forward for medals."

Jane recognised the DSC on his breast. "You must have done something pretty special yourself. Was that Dunkirk too?"

"Yes, but earlier on. I tell you what, are you doing anything later today?"

"I'm due at the French Legation at four o'clock for another clutch of medals. They and the Belgians seem to want to give me something too."

"Good Lord, what else did you get up to?"

"Oh, right at the end I collected a group of very senior officers from a bastion and had some difficulty getting away with Jerries everywhere popping off guns under our noses. They seemed pathetically grateful when my boat got them to Dover so it's more for the collection."

"You even brought the boat back to Dover? That really is something special."

"Well, it was a bit of a mess but by the time I left there wasn't any other way back and anyway it seemed like a neat ending to the trip to return it to where it came from."

He snorted with laughter. "You really are amazing. Was the Navy pleased to get its boat back?"

"Not really. Its battered state was one of the things held against me at the tribunal."

"Yes, I heard that you'd survived a tribunal. They used my RoP as evidence at that. I hope it helped your case."

"They did mention it in friendly terms, that's for sure. Along with the Army's favourable opinions it helped sway them a bit, I think."

Jane had been looking at this friendly officer while they chatted. With straight chestnut hair, cut in a naval short-back-and-sides and startling blue eyes, he was a good-looking specimen. She remembered he was a Lord David something and certainly spoke in the naval version of that frightfully refined way of the upper crust.

"I say, can I come with you when you go to see the Frogs? I haven't anything else on."

"I don't mind but my instructions are only for me. But we can ask them if they'll let you in. Don't you have any family or anything with you?"

"I'm afraid not. My brother Arthur was going to come but there's some flap on at the Foreign Office and he couldn't get away."

"Isn't it rather frowned on for an officer to be seen out with a Wren rating? I'm only a Leading Hand."

"Perhaps, but I doubt if anyone will bother me with that."

He didn't elaborate, but Jane felt a lot went unsaid in that comment.

"Do I call you Lord David, or what? This is etiquette I'm not familiar with."

He roared with laughter. "Good heavens, no. Plain David will be fine."

Jane surprised herself by simpering ever so slightly at this. As they left the Palace they heard a major aerial battle going on away to the East, planes snarling and shooting and the sound of bombs exploding. "The poor old East End is getting it again. I suppose they'll come this far eventually." What neither knew was that one of the biggest daytime battles of the blitz was being fought out in the skies South East of London that day. Although it was honours even in numbers lost, the Germans took the bigger battering and were driven off without doing much damage on the ground. For the rest of the blitz their bombing very largely became a nighttime business.

All of which meant that when Jane emerged from her taxi at ten to four their driver was getting nervous and Jane was glad she had company. It took five minutes to explain that company to the Sergeant at the door, but using her by now slightly rusty French Jane managed to get David into the back of the room. He spoke to her in fluent French. "I didn't know you spoke French."

"You didn't ask me either. But you're not bad yourself. Did you spend time there too?"

He nodded. "I was sent to a French school for a year between Eton and Dartmouth. There are advantages to being a younger son; we get more latitude about what the family expects of us."

This conversation was getting really interesting, but a French Equerry shimmered up and asked them to come to the next room. David was directed to a seat at the back and Jane led to the front of a substantial crowd where she saluted and came to attention. She recognised no few of the officers she had collected from the bastion. A senior Admiral stepped forward. "*Mam'selle* Beacon, it s our great pleasure and privilege to welcome you here today. We feel we owe our freedom and perhaps our lives, to you and it is our honour to recognise your bravery today." He went off into a flowery five minute peroration about the magnificence of young womanhood and how this ceremony would herald a new age of alliance between our great countries. France's recent occupation was not mentioned. Jane could only stand and wait. The Admiral then apologised that some people who should have been at the ceremony were away trying to capture Dakar. The Free French under General De Gaulle, with British naval assistance, had assaulted the West African port a few days before, confidently expecting the French garrison to switch its allegiance from Vichy. But they were wrong. The attack had been strongly repulsed and the whole expedition was failing rapidly. However, the ranks assembled in London were determined not to let their worries about the failure spoil Jane's day.

"*Eh bien, Mam'selle,* now we come to the important bit. It is with the utmost pleasure that the Free French Government invests you as a *Chevalier de Legion D'Honeure* and in recognition of your bravery we award you our *Croix de Guerre*. He took the medals from the cushion a matelot was holding, pinned them on below her British medals then seized her shoulders and kissed her cheeks one, two, three, four times. Jane took a step back but didn't have a clue what to say. "*Merci M'sieur*" and a little curtsey seemed a bit inadequate but seemed to satisfy them. A Belgian General stepped forward to take the Admiral's place. "*Mam'selle*, Belgium is also honoured to mark your bravery today. It is my great pleasure to invest you with our *Croix de Guerre* as well. And Belgium is unique in having a medal especially for brave women who have helped our military people. It is the Medal *De La Reine Elisabeth* and this is the first time the Free Belgian Government have awarded it in this conflict." These were pinned on next to the French medals and again Jane found herself firmly bussed four times on the cheeks.

"Now, would you care to join us for a little celebration?" Jane could hardly say no; she and David were swept into the anteroom where a table seemed completely covered in champagne bottles. A glassful and some *langues du chat* were pressed into her hand and blessing her French exchanges she knew to dip them into the champagne. One unfamiliar General demanded, rather sharply, to know why David was there. Jane found herself a bit tongue-tied and was glad when David cut in, explaining that he too had been rescued at Dunkirk by Jane and had also been at Buckingham Palace, earlier in the day. "Quite the heroine, aren't you," the General remarked and it didn't sound like the fulsome tribute the others had offered. But he seemed satisfied and drifted on. By seven o'clock a rip-roaring party was in full swing and Jane was rationing her drinks with some caution.

CHAPTER 19

At First Sight

It was a splendid party, but Jane had not had any lunch and was feeling a bit wobbly. She mentioned this to David who said, "Come on then, let's have some dinner." With consummate ease he excused them from the Gallic throng. In the taxi she asked, "Where are we going?"

He grinned and said, "The Savoy."

"Wow, that's a bit upmarket isn't it? Do you go there regularly?"

He laughed, shook his head slowly and said, "Well yes, actually. Since we sold the town house in '38 we have simply taken a suite at the Savoy whenever we need a London base. That saves a lot of money and eating there is a bit like my own dining room."

It was starting to dawn on Jane that this naval officer she had rescued was a bit different. Cautiously she asked, "Are you gentry?"

"Technically, I think you'll find we're aristocracy actually, but in these modern times we don't make an issue of it. Pater's a Marquis. I'm the third son, so able to live a reasonably normal life as far as the Navy will allow. The Earl has to be much more conformist, poor fellow. Strictly I'm Lord David Daubeney-Fowkes, but I prefer not to make an issue of it and I'm happy to be plain David to people I know."

"Good heavens, perhaps I'd better retreat now. I don't think a doctor's daughter, even a successful one, can compete somehow."

"Don't be silly Jane. You know your manners and I am really enjoying your company. At least have dinner with me, why should we both dine alone for some outmoded concept of position in society?"

This conversation was getting really interesting when the taxi driver asked, "Ere, are you two goin' to get out of my cab? You've been starin' into each other's eyes for several minutes since we arrived here. Come on, there's another fare waiting."

With the Blitz raining bombs over large parts of London, the Savoy had closed its regular restaurants and rebuilt a cellar space with heavy beams and supports to ensure it could withstand anything less than a direct hit by a large bomb. Coming into this subterranean space with their medals gently clinking was another new experience for Jane. David greeted the headwaiter in French as a long lost friend; this august gentleman bowed exactly the right amount and asked, "Is the young lady dining with you?" Like all such people he had immediately taken in Jane's rating status.

"Yes she is, Georges. Remember I told you about a Wren who saved my life at

Dunkirk? Well, this is the girl who did it."

Georges' eyes opened wide. "Indeed, sir. In which case we are honoured to have her with us. Please come this way, miss. I see from your medals that other countries also appreciated what you did."

Jane gave him the lopsided, but sweet smile that was now a characteristic and replied in her best French. "Well, your generals did, anyway." Georges cocked his head and looked approving, *"Mam'selle parlez Francaise?"*

"Oui, bien sur."

Immediately, she saw positive mental adjustments being made.

They were being ushered to an intimate alcove when a bellow from another table stopped them. "David, come and say hello."

To Jane's horror this came from a red-faced old Admiral with a battleaxe wife beside him. David right wheeled and went across to him. "Good evening sir. I see you're home from sea."

"Yes indeed. Their Lordships decided I'd had enough of the frozen North and relieved me two weeks ago. Can't say I am sorry. Good to see you're well again. Have you an appointment yet?"

"Not so far sir, although there's a hint I might get my first command. Incidentally sir, might I introduce Leading Wren Jane Beacon? She's the young lady who rescued me at Dunkirk."

Jane had been trying to hide, but found herself thrust forward. The Admiral was sitting without his cap on so she couldn't salute him. A quick compromise was a little bob of the knee, which she was finding very useful in acknowledging seniority without making a show of it. The Admiral surveyed Jane in that very naval way, slowly up and down taking in the medals but betraying no emotion. His wife looked frosty. Then suddenly, he guffawed with laughter, stood up and seized Jane's hand, shaking it vigorously. "Delighted to meet you, young lady. You haven't half caused trouble over at Admiralty Arch."

Jane looked confused. "I'm sorry sir, I don't understand."

"There was the most almighty row about what to do with you. Old Buffy is still trying hard to get you chucked out, but the rest of us were so entertained by the whole story that we felt it would be a bit unkind to dismiss you. Best adventure I've heard in years. I'm pleased for your sake that's a majority view among us."

Relief, surprise and some resentment warred in Jane's mind. Had she done what she had only for entertainment value?

"I only did what I felt was right, sir."

"Yes, so I believe. Initiative like that is to be commended, but let me advise you, young lady, to use it with a bit more discretion. Old codgers like Buffy will always take against you waltzing off on your own if you make a habit of it. I was talking to your godfather George last week and he seems to think you're destined for great things, if only you can keep out of trouble. David, you've got a good one there. Take care of her." And with that they were dismissed.

Seated in their little alcove Jane asked, "Who on earth was that?"

"Admiral Sir Joseph Penrose. He's a real fighting admiral of the old school and approves of people who take the initiative to fight the enemy. I don't think he cares who the enemy is; just get in there and scrap with them. So, you're approved of."

"I suppose I should be relieved, but he is a bit old-fashioned, isn't he?"

"Not really. Did you notice how he didn't mind a female being a hero? The Buffys of this world hate you simply because you're a girl. Old Black Joe is more broad-hearted than that. And what's more he has a daughter who is an ordinary Wren, so he doesn't automatically see you coming from the lower orders."

"I came across a Captain Gribben who was like this Buffy. Tried to get me chucked out because I was a girl."

"Good God, you crossed swords with Gribben? Dreadful man. How did that happen?"

Jane had to explain about the trip up the channel in *Amaryllis* and their un-scheduled call at Haslar. With that tale told, David asked, "Who's the godfather that Black Joe referred to?"

"Oh, Rear-Admiral Rodmayne; part of the Naval Mafia from Guzz."

"Jane, you're holding out on me. You're not really all that low down the scale, are you?"

"Yes and no. Although father has been out for years the Navy still plays a strong part in our lives. I suppose you'd call us comfortable middle class, certainly not even minor landed gentry."

David winked at her. "You'll do for me." He ordered for them and the conversation flowed freely. Jane couldn't take her eyes off this delightful man, so at ease in these surroundings. The headwaiter kept an eye on them with an amused smile hovering on his face and the evening seemed to fly by.

"How would you like to go dancing now?"

"David I'd love to. Presumably, you know somewhere that we can at this hour?"

"My dear Jane, at this hour they are only getting started. Let's go to the Cafe de Paris; Snakehips Johnson has the band there."

Jane had a feeling of being a real country bumpkin. All this was an unknown world to her. "Snakehips Johnson? Sounds a bit wild to me. But I'll give it a go."

David leaned back and called, "Georges, hail us a taxi would you?"

The bombing seemed much closer as they made their way across the West End but they ignored it. When they arrived, her escort was greeted in familiar fashion by the doorman, and somehow a table on the edge of the dance floor was found for them. The women, Jane noted were in elegant evening gowns making even her best uniform seem heavy and dowdy. But her scarred face and the bevy of medals pinned to her breast told a different story and when they took to the dance floor the West Indian band broke into, *See The Conquering Hero Come,* much to everyone's amusement. Jane was delighted to find that David was an excellent dancer, light on his feet and commanding without being forceful. He smiled into her eyes, "This place might be new to you, but you've done plenty of dancing, haven't you?"

"I've always loved it and I might have been a ballet dancer if I hadn't grown so big. You're not so bad yourself." From there they got adventurous and tried some tricky steps in the corners; it all worked and for the first time in ages Jane lost herself in the pure pleasure of twirling round the floor. During a slow number in which they really got quite close Jane remarked, "I haven't enjoyed myself so much in a long time. It would be lovely to do it again sometime."

"Why sometime? Let's do it again tomorrow night. Have you a gown with you?"

"Yes, one which might just about do for this place!"

Snakehips, who had been living up to his name by his gyrations in front of his orchestra, called for a Charleston. By 1940, it was being seen as old-fashioned, but still a lively and – if you were inclined – an adventurous dance. "Let's have a competition," he called, "see which lady can do it best."

Immediately, there were a dozen women on the floor throwing themselves around. Dear me," said Jane" is that the best they can do? Shall I show them how?"

"Go on, that could be fun."

And with that she got up and started to move. But a heavy uniform jacket with medals swinging free was a bit of a hamper so she took it off, peeled off her tie and stiff detached collar and let loose. Ten minutes later she had the place in uproar, throwing in a bit of can-can as best a straight skirt would allow. She hadn't noticed she had the floor to herself, so absorbed in the dance had she become. Finishing, there was a roar of approval and applause that went on for some time after she had returned to her chair hot and flushed but triumphant. David gave her a hug of approval and remarked, "Y'know, at times there on the dance floor I could see the Wren who rescued me. The same fierce determination, the same 'what the hell' attitude."

Jane laughed, "Thank you kind sir. I must admit that once I let rip I can lose all sense of control." He cocked an eyebrow at that one.

A new bottle of champagne arrived at their table with a note; *Congratulations young lady. A heroine in many different fields.* It was initialled R C.

"Who's that?" she asked.

"Probably Randolph Churchill; he always has an eye for a good-looking girl."

"And I only have eyes for you. Hope he doesn't mind."

David laughed. "You really shouldn't say things like that, y'know? A chap could get ideas."

'Feel free' she thought to herself, but simply smiled.

The champagne drunk, they left. "What shall we do now? It's only two in the morning."

"Let's walk down to the riverside." They stepped out into a full-blown air raid. Aeroplanes droned overhead and the crump of bombs going off was a lot closer. Fires were burning nearby. Between the fires and the moon they found their way down to the embankment despite the blackout, chatting as they went.

Suddenly he asked her, "do you have a dog?"

"I'm afraid not. I seem to be forever on the move so it wouldn't be kind to keep any pet. We do have plenty of livestock about the place, though. Pappa Gianni our outside man had a dog and a pig and chickens and our cook Eunice has a cat. It was such a shame when they shipped Pappa Gianni off to Canada. The poor old man was the most harmless Italian you could ever come across. Now Agnes is stuck with looking after all the livestock."

"Y'know, Jane, that simply says it again. How many servants have you?"

"It was eight before the war, but one way and another we're down to three old retainers now."

"All this mock modesty about only being a doctor's daughter, really is nonsense isn't it?"

Jane felt this was going in the wrong direction so asked, "do you have a dog?"

"Not a personal one, but there are always labradors about the place."

"Dare I say 'typical'?"

He laughed, an easy intimate sound.

"I doubt if I could stop you."

"No, but servants or not, we're not landed aristocracy."

By now they had arrived at the riverside and were leaning over the wall, looking at the silver ribbon of river. Despite the air raid boats were steaming about on it. Tugs hooted; a sailing barge ghosted silently down on the tide. A flat iron collier pushed its way out from Waterloo Bridge and in the midst of it a naval skimmer went roaring past at high speed. Away to their right, Pimlico and Victoria were getting a beating and the Houses of Parliament were well ablaze. Although they didn't know it, this was the beginning of the end for the old Palace of Westminster as the seat of government and the beginnings of the full intensity of the blitz. Parliament was restored this time only to be bombed to a burnt-out wreck some months later.

They took in the scene for a minute, until David abruptly turned to her. "Jane, what do I care if you're not an old landed family? Just being with you is enough."

For some unaccountable reason she found her knees going weak and was having difficulty breathing. She looked at this sprig of the aristocracy and saw a good-looking young man who appealed to her enormously. Suddenly even speaking was difficult. Instead of her usual cool mezzo voice, she found herself speaking in a breathy squeak. "I bet you say that to all the girls."

He shook his head, bemusement across his face. "Jane, I've never said it to any. You are special. It's not only the history between us. It's – it's – I don't know. But I do know that being here with you is the most magic thing I've ever known. Would you mind if I held your hand?"

'And the rest' she thought to herself but simply said, "It would be nice if you did." And held her hand out. Hand in hand they slowly strolled along the embankment. The aerial bombardment had now ceased and a breathless hush lay over the city. Around them fires raged and to the East a red glow marked where the main attack had come. "Poor old London," she remarked.

"There's worse to come if what I hear is anything to go by. Hitler is determined to try to break the people's morale by bombing us out of our homes."

"He won't succeed. Where is home for you?" she enquired.

"Oh, North side of the Chilterns. The pile is near Leighton Buzzard. How about you?"

"Oh, West Country. We live on the Yealm near Plymouth. But father's Scottish."

"Really? Is he from one of those Scottish medical dynasties?"

"No, his family are farmers in Buchan. Do you know where that is?"

"Yes, I think so. Not shooting country is it?"

"Not really, rich arable territory. Our family has one of those big farms known as farm towns, about five thousand acres."

"That's a lot of farm."

"I suppose so, but not the same as yours, is it? And father has rather broken away from it with his love of the sea and devotion to his medical calling. He was at Jutland, y'know."

"So was my uncle, I wonder if they met. We must compare notes sometime."

By now they had reached Blackfriars Bridge, turned around and strolled back, feeling sleepy but not wanting to break the spell of the moment.

"David, isn't this lovely, I don't want it to end, but I do have a lot to do tomorrow, I mean today now. I have to report to the Wrens' Director and she's a lovely lady but not to be trifled with so I really ought to be fresh. Would you mind if I go back to my hotel now?"

"Jane, anything you want. I'm your slave. I'll walk you back."

Jane's practical nature popped up for a moment. "David, really. You're my slave indeed."

But suddenly he swung round, embraced her and buried his head in her shoulder, dampening it with the odd tear. "Jane, Jane, I've never met anyone quite like you. Please let's stay together. In this ghastly war you never know how long you've got and suddenly I've found someone too precious for mere words."

Jane struggled to stay upright. Her legs had gone, her innards were a melting mess and her throat a dry blockage. Drawing a ragged breath she said, "David, darling, yes, please let's stay together. I can't think of anything more wonderful." And she hugged him fiercely. "You can kiss me if you like."

To her surprise he didn't have a clue how to kiss, simply squashing his damp lips against hers. 'Now there's something he'll have to learn' a detached bit of her brain thought.

They walked on slowly to the Charing Cross Hotel. "I'll pick you up at 1830 here ready for an evening out. I'm having dinner with my brother Arthur but I'm sure he won't mind if you come along too. You don't mind him being there too, do you?"

"No, David, of course not. I'd love to meet your brother." He nodded and turned away abruptly. In the dawn she picked up her room key, hung her uniform up carefully, set her alarm for three hours' time and was asleep in seconds with a deep smile on her face.

CHAPTER 20:
The Lion's Den

Nine o'clock came all too soon and groaning, Jane scuttled down the corridor, had a quick bath and pulled on her uniform again, struggling as always with the studs and the stiff detached collar. Clean, fully dressed and medalled she grabbed a quick plate of cereal then hailed a cab. The Admiralty was almost within walking distance in the time she had, but with Chief Officer Currie's, "Don't be late" ringing in her ears, she was desperate not to take any chances. Arriving at ten o'clock in the entrance she found it was as well that she had allowed plenty of time because security were deeply dubious about her and it took half a dozen phone calls before she was allowed through, escorted all the way by a messenger. She suspected they didn't quite believe the medals. The Wrens headquarters office proved to be somewhat of a let down, pokey and crammed with women behind mounds of paper. No-one paid any attention to Jane as she came in. Confused and uncertain about what to do, she approached the back of a young third officer. "Excuse me," said Jane tentatively. The third officer turned round and it was, "Good heavens, Merle! What are you doing here?"

"Jane! Good to see you. I'm doing administrative and legal stuff and pushing on with my training for solicitor. How nice to see you, Jane. I'm glad we managed to sort out your medals. They look very impressive."

Jane looked puzzled. "Sort out my medals? I don't understand."

"Well, the Admiralty were not keen to give you anything other than the order of the boot, but the Director asked me to see what I could do and I managed to persuade them that loosing you to the Army was not a good idea. So, because the Army were determined to give you their medal and very keen to make a heroine of you, the old Admirals down the corridor were persuaded to give you an equivalent and keep you to spite the Army. But you should be very grateful to the Army. Without them you'd have been out on your ear. It took me a lot of charm mixed with heavy arm-twisting to fix it."

"You fixed, it Merle? Well thanks, but of all people why you? I'd have thought you would be glad to see the back of me after the way I'd treated you."

"Oh, come on Jane, we dealt with that one long ago. You can't help being the way you are and I decided then to accept that and not bear a grudge."

Jane gazed at Merle in wide-eyed disbelief. "This really is a surprise. And now your letter makes sense. At the time, I felt there was a sub-plot in it, but I didn't have time to think about it. Now I understand. And you fixed the Frogs too?"

Merle laughed. "Yes, Jane, I wondered if you would take the hint. Anyway, it's all sorted out now and I'm delighted to see that chestful you've got. The only problem with our French colleagues was restraining them. They wanted you in months ago to pour everything a grateful nation-in-exile could produce onto you. While I was at it, I obtained full permission for you to wear the foreign awards so you can put up those ribbons too. From now on I have a little responsibility to keep an eye on your career, so please, do you think you can try to keep out of trouble?"

"Why do people go on saying this? I never set out to make trouble, only to do my job."

"Ah, but the trouble with you, Jane, is that you don't think what you do will cause any problems, but unfortunately the Navy sees it differently. They are used to people staying in their pigeon-holes and you keep popping out of yours. Anyway, it looks like the Director is ready to see you now."

Escorted by Merle, Jane entered the inner sanctum where she found the Director and also Chief Officer Lady Cholmondley who had been part of her tribunal. They were wearing their hats so Jane came to attention, saluted and reported in official form. Salute returned, the Director gave Merle a nod of dismissal, took off her hat and indicated to Jane to sit opposite her. There was a longish silence while the Director gazed at Jane, took in the medals and smiled gently. Eventually she spoke. "Well Beacon, congratulations on being as extreme as ever. Heroine or out. You have a lot to thank Third Officer Baker for because she really has gone to a lot of trouble on your behalf. It is just a shame that the Navy is insisting on this being done quietly, which means we are not allowed to shout about it; that would have been nice. But that's the price of having any recognition at all and at least we've managed to hang on to our stormy petrel. I've heard stories about your trip to Dunkirk and read the citations but are they really all true? And what's this about a donkey?"

Jane made a hasty calculation that there was no point in holding back and for twenty minutes she regaled the two ladies with tales of derring-do and dodgy moments on the beaches. Apart from the donkey, the retreat with the last of the rear guard in an overloaded boat and under fire seemed to make a particular impression. The Director turned to her winger and said, "There you are, I don't suppose their Lordships will change their mind in a hurry but our danger-lover here has demonstrated that our girls can be effective even under fire. Maybe something to use at some stage."

She turned back to Jane. "Now, a rating with a chestful of medals is still a rating and you will have to remember that. Wren officers still have authority over you."

Jane looked puzzled. "I don't think I've given any trouble that way, ma'am.

Mostly I only do what I'm told."

The Director snorted derisively. "For as long as it suits you, you mean. One thing is clear, the concept of Wren boat crew is now positively and firmly on the agenda. Obedience is a different matter, but already we've been able to persuade their Lordships that girls are capable of handling boats. Wren Johnson is reported as doing brilliantly down at Dover, incidentally."

Jane couldn't help but butt in. "Oh, that is good. I'm not surprised, in many ways she's better at it than I am."

"Quite so. But not so argumentative."

"But Ma'am, but ma'am...."

Lady Cholmondley shook her head sadly and laughed. "You haven't changed, have you Beacon? You were exactly like this at the tribunal."

"Yes ma'am, but if I hadn't stood up for myself I'd have been chucked out, now wouldn't I?"

"That may be so, but it doesn't make you any less argumentative."

The Director cut in. "I did not ask you to see me this morning to discuss your attitude, which I think we all know about already. Your remarkable progress has certainly made a lot of people pay attention who would rather they did not have to. This is doing the cause of boat crew Wrens a lot of good, but at the price of some senior officers swearing that they will get you at some stage. We will do our best to pull a cloak over you, but you will help that process enormously if you stop arguing and dashing off on your own. Is that clear?"

Jane wanted to launch off into a justification of her doings, but felt that it would only re-enforce their view of her. So, she simply nodded.

Lady Cholmondley cut in. "Where did you learn to argue like that, Beacon, or is it instinctive?"

"I was President of the debating society at Leadown School, ma'am and in a big family I've always had to stand my ground, which I suppose contributes."

Lady Cholmondley looked suitably impressed and said, "That accounts for some of it, anyway."

The Director cut in again. "Right. It seems to us that there is not much more to be gained by your staying at Dover. Superintendent Welby is prepared to have you back at Plymouth where her lobbying for Wren boat crew is getting some real traction now. But Superintendent Carpenter at the Nore is also very interested in you and we feel that might be a more productive use of your talents. It would mean running boats on the Thames, which are getting busier and we'd like to introduce you to a Mr Herbert. He's an MP but also a keen boater and wants to see much more boat work on the Thames. We've given him a little of your story and he is fascinated, so perhaps that may be where you can go next. You're due a few days leave, then back to Dover for now, but be ready for a draft by the end of the year. Any questions?"

"Can Wren Johnson come with me? We make a super team now."

"We're tempted to appoint her on her own, but for now she can come with you. But it won't be long before she goes her own way, I rather think."

"Oh, that will be good, ma'am. I don't think I have anything else I dare ask at present."

"All right Beacon, congratulations again on your decorations and do try to keep out of the way of their Lordships."

And with a nod the interview was at an end. Jane retired to Merle's desk and sat down with a sigh. "Was that so terrible?"

"No, not really, but simply sitting across a desk from her is scary enough. I'd hate to get on the wrong side of her."

Merle grinned. "I've seen it happen and it's not nice. Now, Jane, how much do you know about your medals?

"Not a lot, have you been investigating?"

"Yes, I have although I have to say I knew nothing about the MBE. That was a complete surprise, which I suspect may be very useful in keeping their Lordships off your back. To sack someone who has been singled out like that by Churchill and the King, would look very dodgy and I've found out that it took a lot of behind-the-scenes wrangling by Churchill for it to be awarded to you. Remember that having him on your side is not necessarily a plus point with senior officers who consider him a meddling nuisance. Now, you don't wear the medals themselves except on ceremonial occasions. But you do sew little ribbons on your jacket for each medal you've got. I've done a check sheet of what to do and where to get the ribbons. Here it is. A quick phone round this morning tells me that as the MBE is an order, not a medal, it goes above the others. Which means you'll have three rows; MBE, British bravery medals, then the foreign ones."

"Yes, I've seen the ribbons on officers' uniforms, so I do the same?"

"That's right and I bet it gives them a surprise."

Jane grinned at the thought. 'What would Gribben have made of them?'

"There's one other thing, Jane." And Merle produced a length of woven gold strip. "This is wound stripe. It was common in the last war but was dropped in the nineteen-twenties and hasn't formally been re-instated yet. But I managed to persuade the powers above that you should have some in recognition of your outstanding efforts even after you'd been injured. I don't think it is official but you are being allowed to put it on your uniform. It sews onto your left sleeve forearm in two-inch lengths and you're being allowed two stripes on each of your uniforms. There are

CHAPTER 20: The Lion's Den

quite strict regulations about how it is put on so they're on the check sheet as well."

"This is all very kind of you Merle. You've really gone to a lot of trouble for me, haven't you?"

It was Merle's turn to laugh. "I like a challenge and you're all of that. I gather you've also garnered a second Mentioned in Dispatches. How did you manage that?"

"Oh, Wren Johnson and I fished a downed airman out of his burning and sinking Hurricane outside Dover harbour. We were in the skimmer and raced out to pull him free. Unfortunately, he died in my arms, which was tough because I knew the guy. We've rescued English and Poles and even Jerries. I'll bet my shooting a Jerry hasn't been mentioned."

"No, Jane, that one hasn't gone through."

"It's a shame we're not allowed to keep diaries. Mine might be quite entertaining."

"Tell you what, Jane, write to me with your exploits and I'll keep the letters."

"All right, I'll do something once a week and post it away from the military system so it shouldn't get censored. But I warn you that a lot of it is pretty humdrum between times. And not everything I do will go in the letters."

Merle threw her head back and laughed, a cheerful infectious sound that rolled round the ant-heap atmosphere of the over-pressed office. "I won't ask his name, Jane. Did I tell you I've got a steady boyfriend now?"

"No, you didn't Merle. Good luck. Anyone I know?"

"I doubt it, he's a lawyer in the Royal Marines. We met at law evening classes. Tell you what, there's a Lyons Corner House close by. Shall we have a touch of lunch there?"

Lunch with Merle proved to be a lot more cheerful than Jane expected. The third officer lawyer really did seem to have forgiven the earlier ferocity. They reminisced about Probationer Course Two and Jane gleefully passed on what she'd heard about Mrs Brown. Merle politely asked after the state of the bottom almost as though it was a separate entity. Parting afterwards Merle said, "I really mean it Jane. Please make my life a bit easier by keeping out of trouble."

Back at the hotel Jane debated a bit of sightseeing but reaction and lack of sleep were catching up with her. Uniform carefully hung up again and alarm set, Jane flaked out on the bed and was asleep in moments.

CHAPTER 21:
The Real Thing

She hadn't exactly been fat when she bought the petrol blue velvet dress, but trying it on again now it was noticeably looser all round. But it was all she had; it still clung in all the right places and would have to do. As before, she decided to forego knickers to ensure a clean line from end to end. As she dressed and tried some light makeup, David's face came into her mind eye again. He'd rather gone to the back earlier in the day, but with her interview out of the way there was a huge sense of relaxing, of stress draining away and of seeing only pleasure ahead of her. As she thought of him, a wonderful thrill of joy went right through her. 'David, David' she thought and tried it out loud. The name sounded good.

As she came down the stairs a minute early – Naval habits were getting deep into her soul – her throat tightened and her heart gave a lurch on seeing him waiting in the foyer. He did a huge double take at his first sight of her out of uniform. "My God, Jane. You looked good in uniform but seeing you like this is stunning." Jane knew well enough the impression she could make on men, but had never given much deep thought to it. Here was another one, reduced to stammering staring incoherence. But this one was differentl this was her David, sprig of the aristocracy, good-looking Naval officer and the man creating feelings in her that she'd never known before.

"Hello David, nice to see you again." Somehow the trite platitude seemed totally inadequate, but a meeting of their eyes told its own story. He had a cab waiting and in no time they were at the Savoy again. "Welcome to my canteen," he said with a little grin. "Arthur isn't able to join us until seven thirty so I thought we could try the bar first."

"Thanks, I'll have a pink gin."

Settled, he sat staring at her. "I'm sorry Jane, the transformation is so utter, you are so different like this that I can't get over you wanting to be with me; it takes my breath away. I've never seen anything so beautiful."

"You mean my scar doesn't put you off?"

"No Jane, it makes you all the more attractive to me. Knowing the story helps, but even without that you'd still be breath taking." And impulsively he took her hand and held it in both his.

"Y'know, David, you are pretty special yourself."

"Me? I'm only a spare being a junior officer in the Navy. There's nothing special about me."

"There is to me. I think you're pretty special actually."

"Well thanks, but I'm not sure I deserve this."

"David, you don't have to deserve it, just be yourself. There's nothing special about me either, y'know. A doctor's daughter; who is a junior Wren with a chequered history already. You won't do your career any good if it's known you are involved with me."

"Do I care? My career can look after itself and if I have to jeopardise it to be with you then hang the career."

"That sounds very splendid, but I'm not sure it's very smart."

"It's neither, it's simply the way I feel."

She raised an eyebrow and laughed; gently, affectionately.

Suddenly a tall black-haired man loomed up behind David. Lean and bony good looks made him quite noticeable.

"Hello, you two."

David jumped.

"Arthur! I didn't expect you for a while yet."

"Well, we finished earlier than I expected and I decided the routine stuff could wait. Is this the famous Wren?"

David had stood up so Jane decided to do likewise. She drew herself up to her full five foot ten, gave this Arthur her most dazzling lopsided smile and said, "I am indeed the Wren. Whether I am famous or not is another matter. How d'you do." She held her hand out. Now Arthur thought of himself as a man of the world not easily impressed, but Jane at full height and spectacularly dressed had its usual effect. For a moment he could only stare, dumbstruck, before regaining control of himself and taking Jane's hand. "How d'you do indeed. David, you told me about her exploits, but you might have warned me that she was utterly gorgeous as well."

David smiled, "I thought it would be a nice surprise for you."

Arthur fetched a round of drinks from the bar – Jane noted that there was no payment – and they sat down to resume normal conversation. Arthur started. "Jane, isn't it?" She nodded.

"How on earth did David manage to capture you? He's never had a proper English girlfriend in his life. Too shy."

"Really? We just hit it off from the start. Mind you, a burning ship as a shared history did rather melt the ice. It has simply seemed like the right thing to do."

David cut in.

"Jane has made it easy for me, Arthur. She doesn't seem to realise what a wonderful catch she is."

"David, I've told you I'm only a Leading Wren from the middle classes. Don't make it sound like more."

"Jane, how many medals were you wearing yesterday? I think I counted seven, plus two Mentioned in Despatches. An ordinary Leading Wren you are not and breathtakingly beautiful, as well."

Jane was starting to feel that uncomfiness, which caught her when hero worship showed in the eyes of the girls in the Wrennery. She decided it was high time to change the subject. She turned to Arthur, "I believe you are at the Foreign Office?"

"Yes, on the American desk for my sins. I'd like to say 'at least they speak the same language' but they don't really."

At that point, headwaiter Georges arrived to tell them the table was ready, so they finished their drinks and went in. At the door Jane passed Georges and gave him the full height effect. Georges was much too well trained to betray any emotion, but Jane saw his face go red, then white and knew that she had made the hit. The moral voice at the back of her brain said 'Jane stop it. You should not be flaunting yourself like this'. But somehow she wanted to for David's sake.

Once recovered from his initial surprise Arthur proved to be good company and the meal passed in cheerful fashion. The three of them casually drifted between French and English as they went along, using whichever seemed most appropriate. Jane asked, "How is morale among the people? They can't be terribly happy since this blitz bombing started."

"Well, the East End is struggling a bit, because that's where the bombing is and despite Buck House being hit last week, there's a feeling that the toffs are getting away with it while the proletariat take the blows. That could turn nasty if it continues. Hitler would actually do social cohesion here a lot of good by bombing the West End as well. But apart from that there's a strong feeling that we are living through great times making history every day and life really is a precious thing that could be snuffed out at any moment. Plenty of 'we can take it' chirpiness unless you're right under the bombs, which tends to have a flattening effect."

Changing the subject Jane casually asked, "You said you were on the American desk? How are we getting on with our cousins these days?"

Arthur smiled and thought for a minute. "A lot better now Winston has got his feet under the table. He and his Former Naval Person partner-in-crime are rubbing along quite well though they're shamelessly trying to get the advantage over each other. I'll give it eighteen months until they lose their neutrality."

There was a silent pause while the venison was served, then Arthur continued, "David, have you an appointment yet?"

"No, but I'm in with the appointers on Monday and the hints suggest I might get command of a destroyer. That would be fun."

"When are you off?"

"I don't know but I was told to come packed and ready for sea."

Arthur motioned them to come closer. "You know we're getting fifty old destroyers from the Yanks? Well, their Lordships are trying to hurry up the process because they're needed for the convoys and I've heard that any officer in zone will get a step up. Shame you've not got the time in for your brass hat yet."

"I've only been a two-and-a-half for ten months. Long way to go to the great step up."

Jane chipped in, "If only they'd let us I'm sure Wrens could run a ship. Maybe we could take on our chummy ship, *HMS Wren.*"

David and Arthur looked at each other. David spoke. "I told you she was different. Now you see why."

Arthur gave this a cynical curl of the lip but laughed too. With the red mist rising Jane felt cross. "One of these days you men are going to be forced to accept that women can do a lot more than you think and the demands of this war may be the spark to set that going."

Arthur looked startled. "Is that right? I'm not sure I had thought of it like that and what happens to home and hearth?"

"In all probability, we'll have to do two jobs; the traditional one and work for the war effort. You watch out, Arthur, us women are coming."

He looked a bit scared and to save him David changed the subject.

"Arthur, what's the view now on whether the Boches will invade?"

"Well, we think it unlikely. There's a feeling that Hitler is actually up to something else and that all this apparent preparation is simply to throw us off the scent. But no-one knows what that other something is."

Jane chipped in, "Down at Dover it all seems real enough. We get invasion scares every few days, although I suppose they are receding a bit now."

"That's natural, I'd have thought. You are rather eyeball-to-eyeball with them down there."

While all this was going on, Jane and David didn't seem able to avoid catching each other's eye fairly frequently. What was this glow all through her? Why did it feel electric to be sitting next to him? Why did she feel herself blushing when he looked at her?

Coffee and port finished, Arthur looked at them and said, "Well, I've played gooseberry for long enough so I'll push off. Enjoy yourselves, kids." And with a laugh he strolled off. Jane and David looked at each other more closely. Quietly he took her hand under the table. "Jane, what is this? I've never felt this way before. Dare I hope that you feel the same?"

"Oh yes, David, yes. I've never felt like this either. Simply looking at you I feel tingly all over. To be a Lieutenant-Commander you must be a bit older, I'd guess?"

"Twenty-seven now; almost ancient. How about you?"

"David, I'm only twenty. You'll have to ask my father's permission if you want to approach me on port tack."

"Good Lord, I didn't know you were so young. Yet, you seem so mature."

"Do you wonder?" She wrinkled her forehead. "I was a different person after Dunkirk. But being with you now I feel young again."

"Me too, Jane. I had no idea I could feel like this, sort of breathless yet zinging with joy at the same time."

A discreet cough stopped this interesting discussion on world affairs. "Will you be wanting liqueurs, sir? We'll be serving in the bar."

"No thank you Georges, we'll take the hint and move on." He turned to Jane. "Shall we take Cafe de Paris by storm again?"

"Why not? At least I'll be a bit better dressed for it this time."

Somehow they got to the club without noticing their surroundings and despite the bombing creeping ever closer. Settled in a floor side seat again, David ordered champagne, took Jane's hand across the table and looked at her with a pleading, hungry longing. Later, as they danced closely, the band was playing, *The Way You Look Tonight*. They looked deep into each other's eyes as they sang gently to the tune, oblivious to the world around them.

By dawn, air raid finished, they were gently drifting along the embankment again, hand in hand and stopping to kiss and caress at intervals. David looked at her for the umpteenth time.

"Jane, is this love?"

"I think it must be, David, but I've never felt like this before so I have nothing to compare it with."

"In which case, I love you Jane Beacon. That's the first time I've ever said that to a girl and it feels so wonderfully right. My life has changed."

"David, darling, I'm finding it difficult to breath, but if this is love then I love you too. And you're right; everything feels different all of a sudden."

"What is it lovers are supposed to do?"

Jane felt a sudden lurch in her belly. Fear? Excitement? It was hard to tell and was he saying he knew about her chequered history?

"I think they're supposed to kiss and hug, aren't they?"

An enormous sense of relief swept over her as he pulled her into his arms and planted wet slobbery lips all over her face. He went up her scar, onto her nose end, dampened her eyelids. For the moment, Jane didn't mind that, but saw some lessons coming. "David, darling, you haven't done much kissing; have you?"

"No dear I haven't. Why?"

"Because we might be able to make it better. How did your mother kiss you when you were little?"

"Do you know, I don't think she has ever kissed me. She regarded her children as a necessary evil, I think."

Deeply shocked, Jane thought of her own mother. Strict and starchy perhaps, but a loving woman who went round every one of her children morning and night to kiss them awake and to sleep and regarded hugs and kisses in passing as normal. "Your mother has never kissed you? That must have been tough."

"Not really, it never occurred to us that she should. Nanny saw to us until we were old enough to go to school, then we only saw Mater occasionally."

"No wonder you don't know what you're doing now. Arthur said something about you never having an English girlfriend. Is that right?"

He smiled ruefully. "More or less. One or two girls I might have got to know a little better, but the Navy took me away each time."

"You poor man. There's so much I could give you; can you open yourself to me?"

"I think I already have, Jane. This is a wonderful new world for me now."

"And for me, David.I love you, love you, love you David Daubeny-Fowkes. When are you going away?"

"I think Monday after I've seen my appointer. We must write."

"Every day, David dear." She gently started singing again, *The Way You Look Tonight*, with her arms stretched out round his neck, as she swayed slowly and sensuously up against him. All he could do was hang on transfixed, smitten to the core. "I'll remember this song and think of you whenever I hear it."

"All right, it's our song then. Sing it to me every day. I'll send you a photo to sing to."

On Monday Jane, back in uniform, but with medals packed away in their boxes, found a seat in a crowded train, pulled out her pad, and started to write. With several crossings out and pencil chewing, she wrote.

> *David, as we go to our different worlds*
> *We are now quite changed in our hearts*
> *Our souls are open, lie unfurled*
> *To each other in all our parts.*
> *If parting's pain, mem'ry's bliss*
> *It makes me real, it salves my soul*
> *In the pits of longing for your kiss*
> *The very thought of you, makes me whole.*

My love, my love, so far away
My life's point is in our union
Your smiling face is my mainstay
And the strength of our communion.
So, as we go our different ways
Parted by this horrid time
This lonely wait is just delays
Till we meet again in friendlier clime.

On the water is that duty
Which, as ordained, we both must follow
But oh, that water has its beauty
Which mocks the depths of our parted sorrow.
And in the plying of our trade
We see a road, which has no dust
It's the winding path through my heart's stockade
So, until we meet, in you I trust.

My Love

* * *

GLOSSARY

The Andrew   Full name The Andrew Miller, is a term mostly used by the ratings to mean the whole of the Navy's people. Named after Andrew Miller, a particularly notorious pressgang officer from sailing ship days.

AWOL   Absent Without Official Leave; meaning to be absent from a place of duty when supposed to be there.

Bastion   A military term for a strong point or fort within a defensive structure.

Burgoo   The Navy's version of porridge; in previous times this was all that was available for breakfast.

Captain's Tiger   The Captain's personal steward.

Crusher   A naval rating on regulating or disciplinary duty, on shore patrols, or sentry duty.

Cox'n   The Coxwain is the person in charge of a boat.

Guzz   Plymouth and more specifically the Navy's dockyard at Devonport.

Glimping   In the Naval sense, means the male gaze of females, with admiration or attraction.

Hard Liers   The extra payment made to compensate crew sailing in poorer conditions on board old or cramped or rough ships.

Harry Flatters   Absolutely flat calm sea.

Harry Thickers   Dense fog or any other form of poor to zero visibility.

Joss   Good luck; but more than a simple piece of luck. It is a general state of good fortune surrounding a person and their life in the Navy. Term originally from the Chinese.

The Jaunty   The chief regulator on board a ship.

The Jimmy	Or Jimmy the One, the First Lieutenant on a ship. A role not a rank, the Jimmy is responsible for the upper deck and the seamanship aspects of running the ship. In smaller ships, this means the second-in-command.
Jossman	A member of the Navy regulating branch, i.e. the Navy's policemen.
Killick	Leading Rate, the first rate up from a basic Able Seaman and equivalent of a corporal in the Army.
Kye	The Navy's version of cocoa made by shaving off slivers from a solid lump of cocoa, adding a generous amount of sugar, condensed milk and boiling water. Usually made so thick and strong that, "A spoon could stand up in it".
A Mae West	A pilot's floating lifejacket.
Mentioned in Despatches	The first level of commendation/award for a brave or outstanding act. Originates in the reports that commanders wrote after actions, identifying particular people for their outstanding performance.
Mess	The living/eating/sleeping space for the ratings in a warship.
Messing	The catering arrangements for the occupants of a mess.
Oggin	Water, or more specifically the sea.
Oppo	A sailor's closest friend and ally on board. A very old term going back to sailing ship days when the crew were divided into two watches and every member of a watch was allocated a number. The sailor with the same number in the other watch was his 'opposite number' and they shared facilities etc. Long ago abbreviated to 'oppo' and more a social bonding in the modern Navy.
Pompey	Portsmouth.

Pongo	A soldier; the Navy's term for soldiers. The term's origins are disputed and various, but the one the Navy likes best is that "Wherever the Army goes, the pong goes too".
Popsies	Slang, mainly RAF, term for good-looking young women.
Probationer Course	The initial induction course for Wrens when they first join the WRNS. All new Wrens were 'probationers' until they passed this course. They were free to go and the Service could decide not to take them until completion of the course. Commonly abbreviated to Pro Course.
Pusser	The Navy; a portmanteau term for all things naval, as a noun or an adjective.
Rabbit	Things acquired illegally or on the quiet. Not always outright theft, but gained without going through formal channels.
Rum	The Naval rum ration had a vocabulary of its own and it was also a currency. The amount given paid off debts, gave apologies, confirmed friendships or sucked up to more senior rates.
Neaters	A straight undiluted rum, only issued to senior rates.
Grog	Rum diluted with water on a two to one ratio for issue to the lower rates.
Sippers	A small mouthful of rum.
A Wet	A full mouthful of rum.
Gulpers	A large mouthful of rum.
Sandy Bottoms	The whole of someone's ration.
Queens	Anything left over in the rum barrel after an issue, claimed by the Rum Bosun as his perks.
Scran	Food.

Tiffy	An Engine Room Artificer, the Navy's trained and skilled technical ratings.
Trots	Rows of mooring buoys between two of which ships can moor up.
Vs and Ws	A large class of destroyers built around the end of the First World War. Considered advanced when they were built and still going strong in the second war even if considered old and primitive by then. All had names beginning with V or W, hence the class name.
Wardroom	The officers' eating and socialising space in a warship. Officers usually have separate cabins to sleep in except in very small ships where the wardroom also provided sleeping berths.
Whales on a raft	Sardines on toast.
Wrennery	Accommodation ashore specifically reserved for Wrens.
WRNS	Women's Royal Naval Service.

ABREVIATIONS and ACRONYMS

AB	Able Bodied Seaman
ARP	Air Raid Precautions
ATS	Auxiliary Territorial Service; The Army's Women's Service
C/O	Commanding Officer
CGM	Conspicuous Gallantry Medal
DCM	Distinguished Conduct Medal
DQs	Detention Quarters, the Navy's prison and correction centre at Portsmouth

HMS	His Majesty's Ship
HQ	Headquarters
MBE	Member of the British Empire. The lowest level of award in the Order of the British Empire, with military and civilian divisions.
MP	Either Member of Parliament or Military Policeman, the Army's police service.
OiC	Officer in Charge/Command. A Wren term for the officer in charge of Wrens.
QAIMNS	Queen Alexandra's Imperial Military Nursing Service. The Army's cadre of permanent highly trained nursing sisters.
QARNNS	Queen Alexandra's Royal Naval Nursing Service. The Navy's equivalent.
PTI	Physical Training Instructor.
RoP	Report of Proceedings, the regular reports Commanding Officers have to submit on their ships' activities.
RSM	Regimental Sergeant Major.
VAD	Voluntary Aid Detachment; a women's voluntary service with wide duties, although mainly nursing auxiliaries
WAAF	Women's Auxiliary Air Force.

EQUIVALENT RANKS AND RATINGS

WRNS	**ROYAL NAVY**
Director	Rear-Admiral
Superintendent	Captain
Chief Officer	Commander
First Officer	Lieutenant-Commander
Second Officer	Lieutenant
Third Officer	Sub-Lieutenant
Chief Wren	Chief Petty Officer
Petty Officer Wren	Petty Officer
Leading Wren	Leading Seaman
Wren	Ordinary Seaman

BIBLIOGRAPHY

TITLE	AUTHOR	PUBLISHER
WOMEN'S ROYAL NAVAL SERVICE (WRNS)		
Blue Tapestry	Vera Laughton Mathews	Hollis & Carter
Britannia's Daughters	Ursula Stuart Mason	Pen & Sword
The Wrens 1917 – 77	Ursula Stuart Mason	Educational Explorers Ltd
The WRNS	M H Fletcher	B T Batsford Ltd
The Story of the W R N S	Eileen Bigland	Nicholson & Watson
Never at Sea	Vonla McBride	Educational Explorers Ltd
Blue for a Girl	John D Drummond	W H Allen
ALL SERVICES		
Women in Uniform	D Collett Wadge	Sampson Low, Marston
World War 2 British Women's Uniforms	Martin Brayley & Richard Ingram	The Crowood Press Ltd
Service Slang	J L Hunt & A G Pringle	Faber & Faber
The Girls who went to War	Duncan Barrett & Nuala Calvi	Harper Collins
Queen and Country	Emma Vickers	Manchester University Press
BOAT CREW WRENS		
I only joined for the Hat	Christian Lamb	Bern Factum Publishing
Entertaining Eric	Maureen Wells	Imperial War Museum
Maid Matelot	Rozelle Raynes	Nautical Publishing Co.
Ten Degrees below Seaweed	Paddy Gregson	Merlin Books Ltd
An intriguing Life	Cynthia Helms	Bowman & Littlefield Inc.
Sea Change	Yvonne Downer	Dreamstar Books
Land Girl to Leading Wren	Lucia Hobson	Hobson Books
WRENS		
Services Wrendered	Sonia Snodgrass AKA Jack Broome	Sampson Low, Marston
Changing Course	Roxane Houston	Grub Street
Wrens in Camera	Lee Miller	Hollis & Carter
WRNS in Camera	Lesley Thomas & Chris Howard Bailey	RN Museum
Love and War in the WRNS	Vicky Unwin	The History Press
Thank You – Nelson	Nancy Spain	Arrow –Hutchinson Authors
Dancing on the Waves	Angela Mack	Benchmark Press
The War Years	'One small Wren' –Lillian Pickering	Athena Press
From Little Ships to Comets	Audrey Iliffe	Self-published

TITLE	AUTHOR	PUBLISHER
WRENS continued		
Bellbottoms and Blackouts	Louisa M Jenkins	iUniverse Inc
Hostilities Only	Brian Lavery	National Maritime Museum
Wren's Eye View	Stephanie Batstone	Parapress Ltd
Secret duties of a Signals Interceptor	Jenny Nater	Pen & Sword
ROYAL NAVY		
Steam Picket Boats	N B J Stapleton	Terence Dalton Ltd
A Seaman's Pocket Book	Lords Commissioners of the Admiralty	
Jackspeak	Rick Jolly	Palamanando Publishing
Not Enough Room to Swing a Cat	Martin Robson	Conway Maritime
The Royal Navy Day by Day	A B Sainsbury	Ian Allen Publishing
Coasters go to War	John de S Winser	Ships in Focus Publications
The Battle of the Narrow Seas	Peter Scott	Seaforth Publishing
True Glory	Warren Tute	Harper & Row Publishing
German Kreigsmarine in WW II	Chris McNab	Amber Books Ltd
The War at Sea 1939 – 1945	Stuart Robertson & Stephen Dent	Conway Maritime
Naval Life & Customs part 1 & 2	John Irvine	Web site
Hold the Narrow Seas	Peter C Smith	Moorland Publishing Co.
Nelson the Commander	Geoffrey Bennett	Pen & Sword
Men Dressed as Seamen	S Gorley Putt	Christophers
On going to the Wars	Godfrey Winn	Collins
The Hour before Dawn	Godfrey Winn	Collins
Home from Sea	Godfrey Winn	Hutchinson & Co.
One Eye on the Clock	Geoffrey Willans	MacMillan & Co
The British Sailor	Kenneth Poolman	Arms & Armour Press
The Lower Deck of the Royal Navy	Brian Lavery	Conway
Dunkirk Revisited	John Richards	Website off-print
The Evacuation from Dunkirk	W J R Gardner	Routledge/Taylor & Francis
Sunk by Stukas Survived at Salerno	Tony McCrum	Pen & Sword
WOMEN IN WARTIME		
Sisters in Arms	Helena Page Schrader	Pen & Sword
Debs at War	Anne de Courcy	Weidenfeld & Nicolson
Jane: A pinup at War	Andy Saunders	Pen & Sword
As Green as Grass	Emma Smith	Bloomsbury

TITLE	AUTHOR	PUBLISHER
WOMEN IN WARTIME continued		
Corsets to Camouflage	Kate Adie	Hodder & Stoughton
Women in Wartime	Jane Waller & Michael Vaughan-Rees	MacDonald & Co
Our Wonderful Women	Cecil Hunt	Raphael Tuck & Sons Ltd
Sisters in Arms	Nicola Tyrer	Weidenfeld & Nicolson
Love Lessons and Love is Blue	Joan Wyndham	Mandarin
The Secret Ministry of Ag. & Fish	Noreen Riols	MacMillan
Britain's Secret War	Chris McNab	Pitkin Guides
What did you do in the War, Mummy?	Mavis Nicholson	Pimlico – Random House
Women in War	Celia Lee & Paul Edward Strong	Pen & Sword
Priscilla	Nicholas Shakespeare	Harvill Secker
Forties Fashion	Jonathan Walford	Thames & Hudson
The WAAF at War	John Frayn Turner	Pen & Sword
A Writer at War	Iris Murdoch	Short Books
The Girl from Station X	Elisa Segrave	Union Books/Aurum Press
Wartime Women	Dorothy Sheridan	William Heinemann Ltd
WAR		
A Muse of Fire	A D Harvey	The Hambledon Press
Love, Sex & War	John Costello	Collins
What Britain Has Done	Ministry of Information	Atlantic Books
The Battle of Britain	Richard Overy	W W Norton & Co
Battle of Britain	Len Deighton	Book Club Associates
The Great Crusade	H P Willmott	Potomac Books Inc
Moral Combat	Michael Burleigh	Harper Press
Lightning War	The Editors of Time-Life Books	
The Second World War in Photographs	Richard Holmes	Carlton Books
All Hell let Loose	Max Hastings	Harper Collins
Blitz Spirit	Jacqueline Mitchell	Osprey Publishing
Home Front	Juliet Gardiner	Andre Deutsch
Britain at War	Maureen Hill	Atlantic World
The Spirit of Wartime	None	Index/Orbis Publishing
The Blitz	Gavin Mortimer	Osprey Publishing
Greasepaint & Cordite	Andy Merrimam	Aurum Press Ltd.
Wartime Britain 1939 – 1945	Juliet Gardiner	Headline Book Publishing

TITLE	AUTHOR	PUBLISHER
WAR continued		
We shall never Surrender	P Middleboe, D Fry, C Grace	Pan Books
Cheer up, Mate !	Alan Weeks	The History Press
Millions Like Us?	Nick Hayes & Jeff Hill	Liverpool University Press
Never Surrender	Robert Kershaw	Hodder & Stoughton
Careless Talk	Stuart Hylton	The History Press
Listening to Britain	Paul Addison & Jeremy A Crang	The Bodley Head
Human Smoke	Nicholson Baker	Simon & Schuster
Home from Dunkirk	J B Priestley	British Red Cross
Forgotten Voices of Dunkirk	Joshua Levine	Ebury Press/Random House
Secret Forces of World War II	Philip Warner	Pen & Sword
Churchill and The King	Kenneth Weisbrode	Viking
PLACES		
Dover at War 1939 – 1945	Roy Humphreys	Alan Sutton
Hellfire Corner	J G Coad	English Heritage
Life in 1940's London	Mike Hutton	Amberley
FICTION		
The Cruel Sea	Nicholas Monsarrat	Cassell
The Seafarers	Nevil Shute	The Paper Tiger Inc
A Wren called Smith	Alexander Fullerton	Peter Davies
H M S Marlborough Will enter Harbour	Nicholas Monsarrat	Cassell
Not so quiet....Stepdaughters of War	Helen Zenna Smith	The Feminist Press
MISCELLANEOUS		
Etiquette for Women	Irene Davison	Chancellor Press
Etiquette in Everyday Life	F R Ings	W Foulsham & Co., Ltd
Table & Domestic Etiquette	Mary Woodman	W Foulsham & Co Lrd
West End Front	Matthew Sweet	Faber & Faber
Gypsy Afloat	Ella K Maillart	William Heinemann Ltd
Since Records Began	Paul Simons	Harper Collins
Careless Talk Costs Lives	Fougasse/James Taylor	Conway
Private Battles	Simon Garfield	Ebury Press/Random House
The War Within World War II	Thomas Fleming	Perseus Press
Breverton's Nautical Curiosities	Terry Breverton	Quercus

About the Author

Douglas J Lindsay was born to the sea. His parents both came from sailor families and when his father went to sea for the duration of the Second World War, his mother followed the ship to its new base at Scrabster on the Pentland Firth, Scotland where the author was born in 1941. His father sailed on the small coaster Drumlough, which the family owned. It ran as a supply ship for the fleet at Scapa Flow, operating up and down the east coast of the United Kingdom. Remarkably, from 1939 to 1945 it was never touched by enemy action. The family lived in a wooden shack on the Scrabster harbour wall and the author's playground was the harbour and ships berthed there until 1945.

Douglas J Lindsay left his public school in Edinburgh soon after his fifteenth birthday and attended the T/S Dolphin at Leith Nautical College before going deep sea in 1957 as a cadet with the Clan Line – a major cargo liner company – operated to Africa, India and Australia. He settled into a merchant shipping career of which the highpoint was being appointed Captain at the young age of 28, on the large ro-ro freight ships of the Tor Line. Later, he worked in the family shipping office before setting up his own ship management business. In 1985, this business went bankrupt and the author and his wife lost everything. They moved to Berkshire where his wife found work as a housekeeper, a position which provided a roof over their heads.

Very new Captain

The author then took up shipping consultancy and with an interest in square-riggers started sailing them intermittently between consultancy jobs. In the 1990s, work as a ship repossession superintendent produced some adventurous moments. The author has had vignettes from his own life published in The Marine Quarterly drawing on his life in the maritime world.

He has had a lifelong passion for writing. His first published piece, in 1965, was titled rather grandly Improvement of Navigation Lights and Signals published in the Journal of the Institute of Navigation. In the 1980s he attended creative writing classes run by John Fairfax and Sue Stewart, who founded the Arvon Foundation. He has written essays, short stories and poetry and many technical reports.

As well as his years in commercial shipping, the author was for many years a reserve officer in the Royal Navy, sailing as watch officer and/or navigator and gaining a thorough understanding of the Navy's ways and mores. It is with his depth of marine knowledge combined with naval understanding that the idea was born for the Wren Jane Beacon and War series of well-researched books about the boat crew Wrens during the war years.

Printed in Poland
by Amazon Fulfillment
Poland Sp. z o.o., Wrocław

54567711R00101